AF481965

"Rekindled Love"

An M/M Gay Romance

Max Hudson

© 2021
Max Hudson

All rights reserved. No part of this publication may be reproduced, distributed, or transmitted in any form or by any means, including photocopying, recording, or other electronic or mechanical methods, without the prior written permission of the publisher, except in the case of brief quotations embodied in critical reviews and certain other non-commercial uses permitted by copyright law.

This book is intended for Adults (ages 18+) only. The contents may be offensive to some readers. It may contain graphic language, explicit sexual content, and adult situations. May contain scenes of unprotected sex. Please do not read this book if you are offended by content as mentioned above or if you are under the age of 18.

Please educate yourself on safe sex practices before making potentially life-changing decisions about sex in real life. If you're not sure where to start, see here: http://www.jerrycoleauthor.com/safe-sex-resources/ (courtesy of Jerry Cole).

This story is a work of fiction. Names, characters, businesses, places, events and incidents are the products of the author's imagination or used in a fictitious manner and are not to be construed as real. Any resemblance to actual persons, living or dead, or actual events is purely coincidental. Products or brand names mentioned are trademarks of their respective holders or companies. The cover uses licensed images and are shown for illustrative purposes only. Any person(s) that may be depicted on the cover are simply models.

Edition v1.00 (2021.01.26)
http://www.maxhudsonauthor.com

Special thanks to the following volunteer readers who helped with proofreading: Bob, E.W. Gregg, RB, Big Kidd, Blue Savannah and those who assisted but wished to be anonymous. Thank you so much for your support.

Chapter One

Evan

Snow never quite made it to the South during the cold months, but Evan found himself hoping for it as he quietly observed the window overlooking the soon-to-be-occupied winter village. Pockets of puddles sank within patches of gravel on the main paths, nestled between wooden posts draped with metal chain-links. The links crisscrossed in neat patterns that proved a proper barrier for the livestock that would eventually arrive.

A host of small buildings rose around the pens—food vendor huts, a gift shop, a Christmas light trail, and Santa's very own cabin where children would flock to meet this year's Santa. To the far right of the path, near the very rear, rested several piles of freshly cut wood. An additional building was being erected, though Evan wasn't yet sure what it would host.

He sniffled as he squinted at the pane, his eyes flitting up to the sky. Clusters of clouds floated through the electric blue sky, rays of sun poking through the clouds to illuminate the ground below. He redirected his gaze to the elderly man sitting behind the desk, the man appearing bespectacled and wise. The black strands of the man's hair sported streaks of gray, the same shades decorating the coarse hairs of his beard.

"We're losing June this season," the man stated while glancing up from the papers on his desk. "It's a shame."

"Just for the season, Delbert," Evan assured. "We can't very well have a pregnant elf running around."

Delbert chuckled, amusement sparkling in his cloudy blue eyes. "You're right about that, Evan. But I hope we can find someone who won't make much of a fuss about the hours."

"It's volunteer work. Who *doesn't* make a fuss about any of it?"

"I'm glad you've come back every year. You're one of our committed regulars."

Evan grinned. "I like doing it. Being Santa brings me a lot of joy."

"You're good at it, too. Almost as good as I was."

"Oh, I could never live up to your legacy, Delbert. You were the best out of them all."

Delbert beamed. "You're just saying that because I'm old."

"Is that so wrong?"

He cackled, the corners of his eyes crinkling and deepening the wrinkles partially hidden by the frames of his glasses. He removed the frames and wiped his eyes, still snickering as he set them on his desk.

He folded his hands. "Do you have an elf in mind for her replacement? Someone suitable?"

"I'm not sure. I could ask the guys at work, but they're all pretty occupied this year. We have a new game dropping on New Year's that we're trying to finish up in time."

"Of course. That makes sense. Well, I'll dig around and see what I can find. I'm sure June has been searching ceaselessly."

Evan nodded. "I mean, no one could possibly replace her. She's been the best elf ever since she started."

"The finest one. She has a way with children. She'll make a great mother."

"I couldn't agree more."

Delbert grinned warmly. "And how about you, Evan?"

"You want to know if I'll make a great mother?"

Delbert broke into a hearty laugh, going hoarse as he attempted to catch his breath. He waved away the joke as Evan joined his merriment. When he had properly caught a satisfying gulp of air, he reached for the coffee mug sitting to the right of his calendar. A quick sip later visibly put him at ease and he continued to hold the mug, using it to gesture as he said, "I want to know why you haven't had children yet."

Evan twitched, though he managed to cover his physical response by shrugging. "Oh, I just haven't met the right person."

"I can understand that. I had all mine so very young. They're all grown now."

Evan smiled. "I bet you enjoyed seeing them grow."

"I did. They were tough children, but I survived them."

"And now, you get to bring joy to other children."

Delbert nodded, nostalgia washing over his pupils. "In a way, yes. But you'll be doing that more than me."

"I've always wanted kids. I don't have any siblings, so I don't have the pleasure of having nieces and nephews."

"I'm sorry to hear that, Evan."

Evan shrugged lightly. Though he wasn't particularly upset over the topic, his heart still skipped a beat. His throat ran dry as he attempted to swallow away the bitter taste of his dreams swept under the rug.

That was ages ago, he thought. Get over it.

He cleared his throat. "So, can I help with anything else? Building? Fliers? Repairs?"

"Well, we're putting together a new attraction: a snow globe cabin. Martin is handling the construction, but I'm sure he could use a hand once the cabin is set up."

"I can do that, Delbert."

The older man smiled warmly. "Always helpful."

"I do my best."

"Don't you have holiday plans?"

Evan nodded. "I do, but not until later in the month. I have plenty of time to spare until then."

"Don't you do anything else? It seems like all you do is work."

"I love my job. I could play video games forever."

Delbert chuckled. "I don't see how you can. I couldn't possibly spend that much time in front of a screen."

"I can handle it enough for the both of us."

"Indeed. Well, I'm getting the schedule set up. Is there anything you need? Anything I can do to make your volunteer time more comfortable?"

Evan waved away the question. "You're doing plenty, Delbert. I appreciate your offer."

"Just let me know. I'm always open to accommodations."

"How's the suit looking this year?"

Delbert rose from his desk, his eyes sparkling as he gestured to a closet on his left and then opened the door. He withdrew the Santa suit and held it out for Evan to observe.

Evan leaned forward while admiring the seam work, reaching to caress the velvet coat that was softer than silk, the fluffy white trim that looked much like cotton candy, and the black buttons as dark and shiny as licorice.

"Incredible," he sighed. "Your wife has outdone herself this year."

"She spent all year improving the design. You really wore it out last season."

Evan laughed. "I had a lot of kids sitting on my lap last year."

"And you'll have plenty more this year. We're expecting almost double our numbers."

"How in the world did that happen?"

Delbert chuckled lightly as he hung the Santa suit up on the coat hanger to the right of the closet. He relaxed into his chair, sighing as loudly as the leather of the seat wheezing beneath his weight.

"Apparently, Charleston has become a hot spot for the holidays," he explained. "I can expect a lot of those people will be bringing their children."

"That makes sense."

"Do you think you can handle it? We can always hire an extra Santa and set you up in shifts."

Evan laughed. "I'm more than capable of handling it."

"If you find yourself in need of a body double, just say so."

"You make me sound like a celebrity, Delbert."

Delbert cackled. "You *are* playing a character. It only makes sense."

"I'll let you know. But for now, I'm more than happy to take every shift."

"You've been doing that for the past five years. I can't tell you how grateful I am that you came along. Few men your age take on the Santa suit."

Evan shrugged. "I've got the beard and the figure. Why not?"

"Oh, Evan. You're far from fat."

"I didn't say *that*."

Delbert nodded. "I'm just teasing you, son. When I was your age, I had a beer gut the size of Louisiana and grays sprouting out of each ear."

Evan laughed and shook his head. "I don't believe that for a second."

"I'll show you a picture! Rose keeps them ready for guests. Would you like to come by later for tea?"

"I would like that very much. But I should be going now. My lunch break is about to end."

Delbert stood up and extended his hand, taking Evan's hand with enough warmth and love to put Evan at ease. The gesture nearly chased away his lingering thoughts about having kids—very nearly.

"Thank you again," Delbert said. "I'll see you later, Evan."

"Stay warm, Delbert."

Evan grinned as he left, grabbing his coat from the back of the chair and swinging it over his shoulders. He walked briskly from the room, down the hall, and out into the chilly afternoon, huffing bursts of white clouds from his mouth. He sank into his sedan, shivering as he dropped his coat into the passenger seat.

One day, he thought as he turned on his car. I'll have kids one day when I meet someone. I just don't know when that will be.

Chapter Two

Harvey

"Winter Festival," Harvey spat while maneuvering the mouse pointer on his computer screen. "I could do without it."

He clicked on the "x" in the corner of the window, closing out his email. The window blanked out of existence, revealing the home screen of his work computer that sported a photograph of the nearby ocean. He studied the hues of pinks and purples occupying the sky, flanking the setting sun. Even his usual joyful image wasn't doing much for him.

"What could you do without?"

He turned to the panel separating his desk from the cubicle next to him. Following the voice was a patch of red hair and a pair of emerald green eyes. A bulbous nose appeared, then ruddy red cheeks decorated with orange-red freckles. The last to make an appearance was the smile of the man peeking over the top of the divider.

"Leo," Harvey sighed. "Are you eavesdropping again? We've talked about this."

"And I thought we talked about you commenting on your thoughts out loud."

"You're such a dork."

Leo laughed as he rested his arms on the divider. He offered Harvey a playful smirk and reached over to playfully push Harvey's shoulder.

"Come on," he beckoned. "Don't be such a grouch. You know I can't help but be nosy."

"And that will inevitably be your downfall."

"Grump."

Harvey rolled his eyes. "Nuisance."

"Aren't all best friends supposed to be that way?"

"I wouldn't know. You're the only best friend I've ever had."

Leo beamed, jutting his chin into the air as he placed his hands beneath his chin. He appeared to be posing for a fashion spread. Even his eyes fluttered as though performing for an invisible camera.

"That's why I'm the *best*," he claimed jokingly. He dropped his pose, returning to his previous demeanor. "Come on, spill it. You can't keep secrets from me."

"The winter thing."

"The festival?"

Harvey hummed, offering a small smile. "I just don't have time for it. That's all."

"Are you sure it's not because you hate Christmas?"

"I don't *hate* Christmas, Leo."

Leo wiggled his brows. "Right. Sure."

"I just have a lot of things to do with my ridiculously crowded family."

"You have three brothers, right?"

Harvey nodded, raising his eyebrows slightly as he glanced at his computer. "Yep, and all three of them have children."

"How many kids?"

"Between the three of them? Hmm...I suppose they have eight kids in total."

Leo whistled. "That's a lot of presents."

"You're telling me."

"And it must be loud."

Harvey gestured vaguely around his desk. "And now you see why I'm so grumpy every year."

"I just thought that was because you were a Grinch."

"Oh, shut *up*, Leo."

Leo cackled, ducking down behind the divider as Harvey playfully tossed a stress ball in his direction. Harvey shook his head as he sank down into his office chair. The wheels squeaked as he rolled across the rough carpet, rocking himself gently.

"God, it's a nightmare," he sighed. "I never wanted kids. And this is why. They're just *so* much."

Leo reappeared. "I don't want them because they're expensive. I could just get a few dogs instead."

"See, that's more reasonable."

"Exactly."

Harvey smiled. "And *this* is why you're the best."

"I knew I would make the cut sooner or later. So, are the kids wanting to go to the festival? Is that why you don't want to go?"

"It's for similar reasons, yeah."

Leo hummed. "Do you want to talk about it?"

"Not particularly."

"I respect that."

Harvey smiled warmly while folding his hands in his lap. He continued to rock himself in his desk chair, listening to the rhythmic squeak of the wheels and hiss of the mechanisms holding his weight.

It's more about my ex, he reflected while trying to retain his professional grin. *I just don't want to see my ex.*

"You know," Leo stated as he retreated into his cubicle. A series of mouse clicks echoed from the other side of the divider. "It says here they're looking for an elf. You could always volunteer for that ticket you got earlier this year."

"Hey, you're not my lawyer."

"No, but I think it would help. You've been talking about how you don't want to pay the entire thing. Don't they offer community service as a way to pay?"

Harvey shrugged lightly. "That might not be a bad idea."

"Assuming, of course, they accept it."

"I could contact my lawyer."

Leo reappeared. "See? I have good ideas."

"But I'll have to be around kids."

"But they won't be *your* kids. And I'm sure all of them will be focused on Santa."

Harvey hummed curiously. "Who is the Santa this year?"

"Don't you already know that?"

"Then, you would know why I don't want to attend the festival at all."

Leo gave Harvey a sympathetic grin. "You can't avoid him forever, Harvey. He's going to be around whether you like it or not."

"I certainly don't like it."

"Well, it shouldn't keep you from getting things done."

Harvey shrugged. "If he's not the Santa this year, then it's fine."

"And how are you going to determine that?"

"I could always call the place and check."

Leo chuckled. "I'm sure it's not a big deal. How long has it been? Three years? That's plenty of time to get over things."

"You would think so."

"Don't let it stop you from living your life."

Harvey shrugged. "I guess you have a point."

"Of course, I do."

"Maybe he's moved on. Maybe he's dating someone."

Leo arched his right eyebrow. "Does that bother you?"

"Of course, it doesn't! That would make me happy. Maybe then he'll get off my back about the whole kids thing."

"You never told me much about why you broke up. Was it about having kids?"

Harvey nodded. "Unfortunately, yes. He wanted kids. I didn't. It was that simple."

"That really sucks. It seemed like you were happy with him."

"I guess I was for a time."

Leo hummed. "Well, are *you* dating anyone? I haven't heard so much as a peep lately about dates."

"I gave up on that last year."

"I'm sorry, Harv. I hope it gets better. Maybe volunteering could put you back out there. You could meet someone like you."

Harvey smirked. "You mean someone who is handsome and charming?"

"I meant someone who is a criminal."

Harvey cackled, wrinkles forming at the corners of his eyes as his face scrunched up to accommodate for his laugh. Leo followed shortly and then rounded the divider, dragging his chair with him.

"That's better," Leo said. "You needed to laugh."

"Thanks, Leo."

"Any time. So, how about it? I could volunteer with you. I make an excellent elf considering my freckles."

Harvey raised his eyebrows. "You'll volunteer with me?"

"Sure. I think it would be good for us both. Hell, I could meet someone."

"I thought you already met someone."

"She's old news. She didn't like how much time I spent playing video games."

Harvey snorted. "See, that isn't reasonable at all."

"I mean, I do miss her calls a lot."

"Well, maybe you'll meet someone who likes to play video games."

Leo's face lit up like a tree full of Christmas lights. "You think so? I bet that would solve my issue. Maybe I should date a guy this time."

"Hey, leave some for the rest of us."

"You know I wouldn't steal anyone from under you, buddy."

Harvey chuckled. "I know. I'm just teasing you."

"Guys are sometimes better about me being bisexual than girls. It can be a lot to deal with, you know?"

"I mean, I wouldn't know, but I believe you. I'm sorry you have to deal with that. It sounds rough."

Leo shrugged. "I'm used to it. People think I'm confused or that I'm trying to hog the dating field when, really, I'm just trying to be happy."

"Well, I hope the next one that comes along is more accepting than anyone in the past."

"I knew you weren't a huge grouch. Thanks, Harvey."

Harvey chuckled. "You're welcome. Let me finish up this task and then we can fill out that volunteer form together."

"Sure thing!"

Leo scooted back to his cubicle, huffing as he struggled to drag his chair. The wheels seemed to be particularly resistant to working, reminding Harvey that much of the equipment in the office where they worked—a healthcare company that based their success on compassion—was outdated and desperately needed replacing.

As Harvey slid toward his desk, he sighed. His shoulders sagged forward and his forehead nearly touched the screen of his computer monitor, causing him to blink rapidly at the pixels now visible on the screen. He shrugged away his defeated mood and sat up straight, opening his emails once more to sort through them.

And when he was finished, he would take on the task of calling his lawyer, hoping that the age-old feelings from the past wouldn't surface.

Chapter Three

Evan

The walls of the cabin stood strong and sure, smelling much like the pine trees they used to be. Evan admired the natural patterns decorating the wood and smiled as he began assembling the shelves, carefully leveling them against the walls to be measured. As he marked where the shelves would be erected, he heard the sound of feet shuffling on the gravel just outside the doorway.

He turned to witness June approaching, her velvet green dress billowing slightly in the breeze. Her brown boots impressed the gravel as she held her round stomach with both hands, her smile nearly hidden by her fluffy red scarf. Her short blond hair tickled the edge of the scarf and flew up around her ears when the wind suddenly blasted her from the right.

She squinted and held up her hand to block her face.

"Phew!" she sighed as she stepped over the threshold and tugged down her scarf. "That breeze would have knocked me over if I wasn't so heavy."

"It's good to see you, June. How's the baby doing?"

She shrugged while observing her protruding stomach. "Well, she seems pretty stubborn about coming out, but hopefully she's out by Christmas."

"A Christmas baby—what a gift to have."

"I know, right? She'll have Christmas presents *and* birthday presents. It's like God wanted me to be covered for the next eighteen years."

Evan laughed jovially, his cheeks flushed from working most of the afternoon. While he set the wooden shelves aside, he swallowed the lump in his throat, the one that seemed to take residence there whenever June was present. It wasn't that she was a particularly bad friend or that her moods swung rapidly from the hormones running through her system, but rather the fact that she could harbor life at all.

And more so the fact that it reminded him of all the ways his previous marriage had failed.

He fixed a smile on his lips as he turned on his boot heel, opening his arms to gently embrace his friend.

"Only eighteen years of gifts, eh?" he teased. "I'm sure it'll be worth it."

"More than worth it. She'll be set with the way Robert saves money."

Evan nodded, keeping his grin. "That's excellent, June. I'm very glad to hear it."

"This place is looking *fancy*," she said as her eyes darted around the cabin. She sniffed the air. "And so pleasant. I hope it still smells like this when we open."

"I'm sure it will. If not, we can always get that fancy pine spray."

"I do love that pine spray."

He chuckled lightly. "We'll be setting the shelves all over the walls and each one will harbor a dozen or so snow globes."

She patted her belly with a sheepish grin. "I feel like I would fit in just fine with the snow globes."

"If it helps, I think you're glowing just fine as a globe."

"Well, thanks, Evan. I appreciate that."

Another set of footsteps erupted from beyond the door frame. It mimicked the shuffling of June's boots, but had its own distinct sound that made Evan twitch with the familiarity of it. He frowned as he glanced over June's shoulder.

"Did anyone come with you?"

"Oh," she said while turning. "I meant to tell you about the new elf. He should be working closely with you."

"A new elf! Finally! Well, no one could possibly replace you, June. You've been one of the best of Santa's elves."

"You're only saying that because you want me to come back."

He laughed and batted his eyelashes. "Is that so wrong?"

"Hey, Harvey! We're in here. Come check out what will be the snow globe cabin."

"Harvey?" he repeated bitterly. "What...?"

His eyes widened as the sound of shoes crunching gravel ceased at the door. Of all the time for the world to spin, his brain chose this exact moment. As his eyes sharply focused, his lips set into a thin line, his jaw clenching as his arms went stiff at his sides. He lifted his chin an inch as though by raising his eyes to the frame above the doorway, he could banish the figure standing there now.

He cleared his throat loudly. "Harvey."

"Evan."

June raised her trim eyebrows between the two men, the excitement once glimmering in her eyes now a distant hum. She pointed to Harvey.

"Have you two met?"

Evan shrugged. "We have."

"Oh, that's great! I was worried that you would have to—"

"Harvey, would you care to explain to June how exactly we've met?"

Harvey looked sharper than he ever had. His chocolate brown hair was short and combed over his forehead, giving him a boyish alternative appearance. His wide-set eyes were typically honey-speckled in the light, but now appeared to be two dark and ominous pools. His facial structure was the same as Evan always recalled, roundish with stubble decorating his cheeks and a wide nose splitting his features evenly. His slim frame was draped with khaki pants, dress shoes, and a winter coat that almost seemed too big for him.

As Harvey flicked his hair away from his eyes, he offered June a cool smile and said, "We used to be married."

"Married?"

"I suppose Evan never told you."

She glanced at Evan, eyes full of confusion. "I had no idea you were married. Why didn't you tell me?"

Evan tried to smile. His best effort was thwarted by a grimace that appeared instead.

"Well," he huffed. "It wasn't important information."

"Of course, it wasn't," Harvey agreed. "I was never quite as important as having children, was I?"

"Don't start, Harvey."

Harvey raised his hands in the air. "I haven't started a thing."

"Should I... Should we find someone else?"

"No," Harvey and Evan replied simultaneously.

She raised her eyebrows again and forced a grin. The poor woman seemed so deeply uncomfortable that she began inching her way to the door.

Evan, noticing how her round eyes sought to determine what exactly to do in this situation, nodded to her and said, "Could you give us a moment, June?"

"Of course," she replied while patting her stomach gently. She offered a gentle smile as she scooted past Harvey. "I'll be in the office."

After her footfalls faded, Evan cleared his throat. He stood awkwardly close to the opposite wall in an effort to put as much distance between his ex-husband and himself. He reached out to caress the smooth wood, the cool surface of it comforting his palm as he applied weight to his hand. The wood creaked slightly.

"What are you doing here, Harvey?"

Harvey took a few tentative steps into the cabin. His hands were tucked deep into the pockets of his parka and his eyes rolled around the cabin, observing everything in sight.

"This is nice. Did you do this?"

"Mostly."

Harvey hummed. "You always were talented with this sort of thing."

"You didn't answer my question."

"I need community service hours. This seemed like a good opportunity for that."

Evan huffed. "I can't imagine you didn't have other options."

"Are you mad that I'm here?"

"Honestly, I am, Harvey. Of all the places, you chose this one. You hate children, too."

Harvey shook his head. "I don't *hate* children. I just don't want them around me."

"That sounds like hatred to me."

"There's a huge difference."

Evan chuckled nervously. "That's not what I remember from our marriage."

"It's been three years, Evan. Why don't you let it go?"

"Don't you think I've tried?"

Harvey stared at Evan for what seemed like a long time. The only sound in the cabin was the wind whipping around the structure, carrying with it twigs, leaves, and soot that patted against the outer walls. A car horn blared in the distance and muted footfalls echoed from the other side followed by the sound of idle chatter.

Evan cleared his throat. "I just don't understand why you're here."

"I made a mistake, got a ticket, and now I'm trying to remedy it without paying a ton in court fees."

"I guess that makes sense."

"There might have been a time where you found that rather resourceful."

Evan shrugged lightly. "I guess I'm having a hard time seeing you as responsible at all."

"I'll take that as a jab."

"It was meant as one."

Harvey broke into a smile. Though he seemed entertained, the right corner of his mouth twitched, a signal to Evan of the annoyance that lay in wait just beyond those delicate lips.

Harvey frowned suddenly.

I used to love kissing him. Now, I can't stand the sight of him, he reflected as a cold sadness crept into his chest. I almost miss it.

He shook his head.

"If we're going to work closely, we should set some ground rules."

Harvey shrugged. "That's fine by me."

"And if you don't like it, you can—Wait, what?"

"I said, that's fine by me."

Evan blinked. "No snide comments about kids. All you have to do is stand to my right when the kids approach to sit on my lap. You can be in the pictures or not. That's entirely up to you."

"That's fair."

"And no drinking on the job."

Harvey twisted his lips as his jaw clenched. "I've got that under control."

"I don't know that for sure, so I guess we'll find out."

"What else? Anything else?"

Evan glanced up at the ceiling, searching it for additional thoughts. He ultimately shrugged and dropped his gaze back to Harvey.

"Smile. As much as you can."

Harvey nodded. "I'll do my best."

"I'm heading to the office. I'll see you later."

Without another word, Evan swept from the cabin and out into the chilly afternoon. He marched with determination to the front office with tunnel vision, attempting to escape the dreadful presence of his previous lover. When he was safely inside the office, he collapsed into the chair near the desk where June was sitting with a novel in her hands.

"*So-o-o-o,*" she drawled out without glancing up from her book. "How did that go?"

"Disastrous."

She closed her book and rested it on the desk, focusing on Evan as she leaned against her elbows. "I'm so sorry, Evan."

"It's not your fault. You didn't know."

"See, that's the thing. We've been close for a few years now. Why didn't you tell me about your ex-husband?"

A snide remark crouched behind his teeth, waiting to snap out until he noticed how confused and pained June appeared. He let the comment fade away as quickly as sand sifting through his fingers. As he cleared his throat, he offered a light shrug.

He sighed. "I was embarrassed."

"About Harvey or the divorce?"

"A little bit of both, admittedly."

She nodded slowly. "Well, I can't pretend to understand, but I can offer as much support as I can. Would you like me to find someone else? He came in with a friend. Maybe his friend can be your elf."

"No, I think it's time for me to get over it."

"Evan, you can take as much time as you need. I know it can be difficult after a break."

He forced a smile. "It'll be fine. I think this is what I need to get over it. He seemed receptive to my ground rules."

"Well, that's good. Can I ask why you two got a divorce?"

"Difference of opinion."

She arched her right eyebrow and smirked curiously. "On?"

"Having children."

"Ah, that makes sense."

He nodded. "I want a family. He doesn't."

"That can break up a relationship real fast. I speak from experience."

"I'm sorry, June. No one should ever have to go through that nonsense."

She shrugged and smiled warmly. "It led me to Robert, so I don't see it as a bad thing. Maybe you two can be friends after this. I'm sure it'll take time, but he seems like a decent guy."

"Yeah," he huffed as he folded his hands and dropped his gaze. "Maybe we *could* be friends..."

Chapter Four

Harvey

After the unpleasantness that met Harvey on Wednesday, he returned to the Christmas village on Friday with every intention to gain the hours necessary to reduce his ticket. He wandered along the gravel path with his hands tucked into his pockets, studying the holiday decor that seemed to have sprung up overnight.

He reached the snow globe cabin and stood just outside, marveling at the electric candles flickering in each window that was framed by garlands. Bells decorated the garlands, nestled neatly among glimmering white lights. He smiled slightly as he stepped toward the doorway and inhaled the warm scent of vanilla.

A memory flickered over his vision temporarily that he did his best to blink away while crossing the threshold into the cabin. He regarded Evan painting the counter at the far end of the room, flanked by two gargantuan trees in desperate need of decorating.

"Where should I start?" he asked. "What do you need?"

Evan perked up from his task, surprised to hear Harvey speak. He stared blankly at Harvey for a moment before nodding to the tree on his left.

"Decorations."

Though it was a simple command, Harvey chewed through it as if he had been tasked to chew through tinsel. He actively loosened the muscles in his jaw as he crossed the room and grabbed a nearby box. He popped it open, withdrew a set of lights, and began stringing them loosely through the branches of the plastic pine tree.

"I half-expected these to be real," he commented as he worked. "I mean, considering the village."

"Budget is low, so we reuse these trees every year."

"Makes sense."

Evan grunted. The sound prompted Harvey to look in Evan's direction, to study the way Evan concentrated. That look was far too familiar. The strands of Evan's reddish-orange beard were strewn with fine brown hairs, giving his beard a thick dimension. His close-set eyes squinted while he expertly guided the paintbrush over the wood, a pink tongue poking from between his thin lips.

The Christmas lights flickered over his features, illuminating his hazel-blue eyes, causing them to shimmer like fine stones. His build was thick and his barrel chest took up much of his t-shirt, sweat stains decorating each of his pits. The reddish-orange hair decorating his muscular arms curled in various places, nearly as thick and lustrous as his beard.

Although the same could have been said for the hair on his head, it was the only hair on his body that was dark. It was styled in a fade with the top combed back, though a lock of hair hung rebelliously over his left brow. When he smoothed it back, it returned to its place, resistant to staying out of his vision.

"Do you need help?" Harvey inquired, turning his eyes back to the tree. "Seems like you might need a headband."

"I'm fine."

"I've got one back in the car. I can get it."

Evan snorted. "I'm having a hard time believing your offer is genuine."

"Why wouldn't it be?"

"Maybe because we're divorced, Harvey."

Harvey rolled his eyes. "That doesn't mean I can't be nice to you."

"I beg to differ."

"Then, I guess you'll spend the rest of your life begging, huh?"

Evan dropped the paintbrush into the bucket, gooey drops of forest green splattering his already stained jeans. He planted his hands on his hips as he turned to Harvey, his concentrated features quickly shifting to hard frustration.

"I could do without your attitude."

Harvey shrugged. "So, replace me."

"We're too short on time for that."

"If that's the case, stop making such a big matter out of such a small inconvenience. Or would you rather I step aside and leave you with all the work?"

Evan grimaced. "You would like that, wouldn't you?"

"I don't think I'm the one with the attitude."

"I've got a short fuse today, Harvey."

Harvey raised his eyebrows curiously. "I can tell. Do you want to talk about it? Maybe getting it out of the way could help."

Resolute in his offer, he dropped the last of the Christmas lights on the tree and turned to face Evan, crossing his arms. He implored Evan with an inquisitive glance.

"Say whatever you need to say," he suggested. "Get it all out so we don't end up bickering in front of the kids."

"I... I don't..."

The look of frustration faded from Evan's face, disappearing as smoothly as the crinkles at the corners of his eyes did when his features relaxed. Soon, his features drooped as did the focus of his gaze. He stared at the floor just in front of Harvey's shoes.

"I don't know how to handle this."

Harvey shrugged. "Neither do I but pretending like we don't have a problem isn't going to make that problem go away. That's how we ended, remember?"

"When did you become so logical?"

"Three years is a long time to think."

Evan met Harvey's gaze, a memory twinkling in his irises. He sniffed loudly, gave a curt nod, and dropped his hands from his hips.

"All right," he sighed. "I think you're a pompous weasel."

"And I think you're a workaholic."

Evan looked mildly amused. "Well, I think you're going to destroy that tree just by being near it with your awful holiday attitude."

"And I think you would shit tinsel if you could."

"If we survive this, I never want to see you again."

Harvey cocked his head slightly to the right. "Deal."

Evan squinted. After a moment, he took a hesitant step forward and extended his hand.

Harvey observed the thick hair on the back of Evan's hand, the waves of lustrous silk pausing just beneath Evan's knuckles. As he reached to take Evan's hand, he felt the breeze billow through the open doorway, ruffling his hair and tickling the hairs on the back of his neck. He met Evan's gaze with a curious wonder, the kind that could have alerted him of an attraction if it hadn't been his ex-husband he was shaking hands with.

He shivered.

Evan raised his eyebrows. "Cold?"

"I'm fine."

"You were always the first one to get cold during the winter."

Harvey chuckled lightly, still holding Evan's hand. "You were always a human heater."

"I suppose that makes me a fine bed partner."

"And who might the lucky guy be?"

Evan released Harvey's hand, shrinking back to the desk. He shrugged slightly as he bent to lift the paintbrush from the can and applied the bulky bristles to the top of the desk.

"No lucky guy," he replied softly. "It's just me."

"I'm surprised by that. I figured you would have replaced me by now."

"Well, you were hard to replace."

Harvey froze as he reached into the box of decorations. The tips of his fingers brushed against a particularly cool ornament, a round red ball with shimmering skin that reflected the warm lights glowing around him. He raised his gaze to the man he had spent years attempting to forget. All the nights he had spent alone in his bed with his arms wrapped right around his wiry shoulders assaulted his brain, causing another shiver to trickle down his spine.

He took a shaky breath. "You must not mean that."

"Mean what?"

"I assume you just mean that I'm hard to replace because there isn't much of a gay scene here in Charleston."

Evan looked like a deer in headlights. His eyes were focused on the tree, yet he seemed inclined to lean in Harvey's direction. When his eyes flicked to Harvey, he shrugged lightly and said, "Yeah, that's what I mean."

"I can't imagine you ever missed me."

"Not a lot."

Harvey snorted. "Same. At least we can agree on that."

But I did miss him, he reflected with a sullen expression as he lifted the ball from the box. He's right—I do get cold first. And every time it gets cold, I think of his body.

"I have an extra jacket, by the way," Evan offered in a low voice that was nearly lost to the whistling wind outside. "It's in the car."

"I'll be fine."

"I can shut the door."

Harvey hesitated, turning with a confused expression before nodding in the direction of the door. Evan completed the offer, cutting off the biting breeze before it could snuff out the vanilla candle sitting nearby.

"You always loved that scent," Harvey commented. "Which means I came to hate it."

"You never liked anything scented."

"I'm a plain man."

Evan chuckled lightly. "You're a *boring* man."

"Hey, at least I was good at other things."

"Like what?"

Harvey took a sharp breath, hanging the ball ornament on one of the prickly branches of the tree.

"Well," he sighed. "I was a good kisser."

"I mean..."

"You can't deny it, Evan. And with your thick beard, I was one of very few men in the area who would even dare to take on the task of kissing you."

Evan's face burned red, his smile turning sheepish as he rubbed the back of his head. Harvey laughed as he went to reach for another ornament, catching one of the branches with the sleeve of his puffy coat. The tree followed him as swiftly as a leash being tugged by an excited dog with no owner in sight. Before the tree could engulf Harvey, Evan snatched the branch and lifted it up, righting it in its place.

"Careful," he warned. "Low budget, remember?"

"Jeez, I'm sorry. I'm still pretty clumsy."

"You always were."

Harvey shrugged as he stood upright to make sure the tree wouldn't fall again. As he reached through the fake branches to grab the center, his fingers brushed against Evan's arm. He gripped the center of the tree and cleared his throat. Evan's hand was within reach. Part of him wanted to grab it, and he almost instinctively did so.

"Clumsy," Evan repeated. "How many ornaments broke that year we had snow flurries?"

"Dozens," Harvey whispered. "We had to go out and buy new ones."

"And you still broke the new ones."

"I can't help that I have an inner ear issue. My balance is off."

He wobbled slightly. He grabbed Evan's shoulder to steady himself, nearly taking Evan to the ground. As he adjusted his stance, he noticed Evan's proximity, feeling the heat of Evan's breath against his cheek. His eyelids fluttered as he inhaled the familiar scent of Evan's cologne—a delightful mixture of cedarwood with a hint of vanilla.

The memory of that scent made him shudder. It compelled him to react in ways he couldn't control, turning to take Evan's lips before he could even think about it. The feeling of Evan's lips made him feel like he was returning home after a long battle overseas. He searched for Evan's hand, taking it eagerly and gripping it as a way to chase away his instant regret. His heart thumped, his blood pumped, and his cheeks flushed as he realized what he was doing.

And he blushed harder when he realized Evan was returning the kiss.

Harvey withdrew, stumbling back. His shoulders met the wall and his eyes focused on Evan, noticing the look of confusion and excitement that reflected his own. He raised his eyebrows curiously, imploring Evan's gaze, searching for the anger that he knew would shortly follow. He had made a huge mistake out of a moment of weakness. He didn't *mean* to kiss Evan.

But did Evan mean to kiss back?

"Sorry," he said quickly. "I just...Well, it's been...I didn't mean..."

"Yes, you did."

Harvey whimpered, "I *did* miss you."

"I missed you, too."

"I'm sorry that I..." Harvey licked his lips, tasting the subtle hint of coffee that had been on Evan's lips. "I should go."

He rushed to get to the door, taking with him the laundry list of reasons circling in his brain of why he shouldn't have taken such a huge leap. But as he reached for the knob, he heard Evan shift. The floorboards, though they were new, squeaked slightly beneath Evan's weight.

Harvey turned around, witnessing Evan's shy grin.

"Maybe we can do that again," Evan said. "Tomorrow. After the festival."

"Maybe."

Evan shrugged. "It's up to you."

"I didn't think you..."

"Well, I do. Call it whatever you want—loneliness, desperation, longing—it doesn't matter. Can we do it again?"

Harvey smiled slow and wide, revealing a row of perfectly straight white teeth. He whispered, "Yes, we can do that again."

Chapter Five

Evan

I didn't think there was anything left with Harvey, Evan considered as he stood in front of the mirror in the office. He adjusted his velvet red coat, tugging the shiny black belt over his gut and fastening it tight. *Am I just lonely or was all of that real?*

"Wow, you look...incredible."

Evan shrugged to adjust the coat as he turned around, hooking his fingers into the spacious pockets of the jacket. The bell sitting in his right pocket jingled slightly. He huffed with amusement as he studied Harvey's outfit: the forest green shirt sparkling every time Harvey shifted, the matching green slacks that led to the pointed brown shoes, and the brown vest with a name tag sporting Harvey's title as Santa's helper.

Harvey held up his hat, the same forest green as the rest of his costume, which hosted a bell at the pointed end of it. He tugged it on his head and held out his arms as if presenting a gift to a friend.

"Well?"

Evan smiled. "You look adorable."

"I look like I'm twelve."

"It's the curse of being a baby-faced gay man."

Harvey laughed. "You look like you could be my daddy."

"Haven't we done that before? During role play?"

"Hush, Evan."

Evan cackled as he switched his attention back to the mirror, pulling the scarlet cap with white trim over his reddish-brown hair.

Harvey appeared in the mirror behind him holding up a bottle of baby powder. "Now for the most convincing part of your costume."

"You remembered."

"Of course, I remembered. It's the same stuff that made me sneeze every time you came home from this damn festival."

Evan arched his right eyebrow. "It's a *damn* festival now, huh?"

"It's a damn *something* that is going to make my ticket go away."

"And here I thought you were doing this out of the kindness of your heart."

Harvey smirked. "Maybe I wanted to see you."

"I find that hard to believe."

"Not after that kiss."

Evan pressed his lips together, causing them to nearly disappear as he stifled a crooked smirk and dropped his gaze to the buckle of his belt. When he raised his gaze to Harvey's reflection, he found a hint of mischief in those dazzling hazelnut eyes.

He turned around and jutted his chin. "Go ahead."

"Ah, I suppose this is part of my duty as your helper."

"It's in the job description."

Harvey chuckled as he opened the bottle and began lightly drizzling powder all over Evan's beard. A plume of powder floated toward his nostrils and he squinted, his eyelids fluttering as he took a step back and raised his nose to the ceiling.

"Pink and purple polka dots!" Evan exclaimed. "Don't sneeze!"

Harvey pressed the back of his hand to his nose. When the near-sneeze had passed, he dropped his hand and shook his head.

"Wow," he sighed. "I can't believe that phrase still works."

"What can I say? It's magic."

Harvey laughed. "You're ridiculous. And I can't believe you even still say that. When did you coin that phrase? When we were ten?"

"It was before our teenage years. Mom used to shout it across the house when she heard me gearing up for a sneeze."

"Your mother was always so sweet and silly."

Evan grinned. "Yeah, she's a good woman."

"I miss her."

"I know you do."

Harvey raised his eyebrows slightly while focusing on the buttons of Evan's coat. He reached out to play with one, adjusting part of the jacket even though the jacket seemed fine by Evan's inspection. After a fit of blinking, Harvey raised his gaze and smiled. His eyes were glossy.

"Are you ready?"

"As ready as I can be," Evan admitted. "Are *you* ready?"

"I took my aspirin. A child can scream in my ear all night and I won't even notice."

"You're a dork."

Harvey smirked and winked. "And you're a nerd."

"Let's get to the cabin before the kids get rowdy."

Evan led the way from the office to the common area of the building. A collection of elves and helpers were gathered around the coffee table, waiting for their cue. Delbert was waiting for him with a clipboard near the door, wearing a pair of khaki slacks and a green sweater with an obnoxiously colorful Christmas tree plastered on the front.

Delbert smiled wide. "Evan! You look fantastic. Let's get the parade going to the cabin. All right, elves! Line up with Santa! Where's Mrs. Claus?"

The elves and helpers gathered around Evan who guided them out of the doors and onto the gravel path. A woman wearing a matching outfit with white curly locks appeared at Evan's side, taking his left arm. Evan procured the large bell from his pocket and began ringing it, announcing his presence as he walked toward the cabin. A long line of children and parents were already waiting for his arrival with Mrs. Claus, flanked by a half-dozen elves.

As he approached his chair, he greeted the children waiting in line, smiling and waving as they cheered excitedly. He settled into his chair, set down his bell, and gestured widely.

"Merry Christmas, kids!"

"Merry Christmas, Santa!"

He let out a hearty laugh, emphasizing his famous phrase of *ho, ho, ho* as a few kids were guided by Harvey to Santa's chair. He pulled one into his lap, asked what they wanted for Christmas, and then posed for a photograph. This process repeated for another couple of hours, never once causing him to lose his spirit or jovial demeanor.

The woman dressed as Mrs. Claus leaned over to whisper into Evan's ear, "We're about done. Want me to get your coffee ready?"

"Yes, Nikki. Thank you."

She smiled and waved to the remaining children before wandering toward the office. Harvey remained at Evan's side with his smile wavering a bit. He nudged Evan playfully.

"I see you've replaced me already," he teased. "With a *woman*."

Mischief danced in Evan's eyes as he said, "Mind your tongue here, Harvey."

Harvey chuckled playfully and patted Evan's shoulder. "My apologies."

"Wow, I've never heard you say that before."

The last of the kids met Santa and went away with their parents to see the rest of the festival. As the photographer began packing up, Evan stood from his chair and stretched his arms above his head. He groaned as he felt the muscles in his thighs and back squeal with soreness. His stiff joints popped. He took a breath, puffed up his chest, and invited Harvey to walk with him back to the office.

The warm air coated his cheeks and made his face burn with the chill of winter weather inside the warm building. Nikki handed him a foam cup filled with coffee and he took a sip, sighing gratefully as the liquid settled in his jolly gut.

"You did well," she praised. "And your helper wasn't bad either."

"Thank you, Mrs. Claus," Harvey said. "You did a phenomenal job."

"If I didn't know better, I'd say you two were close friends. Or even partners. You seemed to work so well together."

Evan choked on his coffee, covering his mouth as he sputtered over an explanation.

Harvey intercepted and said, "It must be the spirit of the holidays."

"Must be," she agreed with a grin. "I'll see you two tomorrow!"

Evan waved as Nikki walked away, waiting until she was gone to shoot Harvey a curious smirk.

"The spirit of the holidays, eh?" he teased. "How about you help me with this suit? My arms are killing me from lifting all those kids."

"You got it, *Santa*."

Evan shook his head as he wandered down the hall to the main office. He shut the door once Harvey was inside, turning to find a pair of lips waiting to pin him in place. He dropped the foam cup that was now half-empty, the sound of it thudding lightly to the ground and interrupting the eager huffs floating from Harvey.

Evan inhaled sharply, welcoming Harvey's cool lips. He cupped Harvey's face and hummed agreeably, each groan echoing back from Harvey's warm mouth. Harvey's tongue poked between his lips and invited him to respond, to playfully push back with his own tongue.

Laughter reverberated beyond the windowpane and reminded him that they weren't alone. He drew back, resting his head against the door as he struggled to open his eyes. He observed Harvey's desirous gaze, lids heavy and eyes affectionately imbibing his image.

"We should relocate," Evan whispered. "Too many witnesses here."

"Sorry, I couldn't help it."

"That's okay. Let's go to my place."

Harvey nodded with excitement. He released Evan, stepping toward the bins behind the desk to gather his things. Evan stood in front of the mirror as he stripped away his costume and carefully hung it in the closet. As Harvey assisted him, he burned with anticipation, wondering if his ex-husband still felt the same after all these years.

How much can one person change? he reflected as he kicked off his black boots. How much have I changed?

After he had changed into a pair of dark blue jeans and a flannel shirt, he smiled at Harvey. He pulled on his winter coat and nodded toward the door.

"Ready?"

Harvey grinned. "Yes, sir."

"Oh, I like the sound of that."

"I'm sure you'll like it a lot more when we get to your place."

Evan smirked while taking Harvey's hand. "I'm sure I will."

He released Harvey's hand before leaving the office, guiding Harvey through the front doors and toward the parking lot. He hopped into his car and watched Harvey do the same, only turning the key in the ignition when he saw that Harvey was ready.

And as the winter wind whistled around his car, he led the way back to his house with Harvey following behind.

Chapter Six

Harvey

Evan's house loomed over Harvey as he stepped up on the porch, following Evan to the front door. He held his breath as he glanced at the living room window to the right, noticing the electric candles flickering gently on the other side of the pane. As he exhaled, he stepped inside the house, glancing around through the darkness until light struck his eyes.

He blinked rapidly while observing the foyer. "Not much has changed."

"I didn't feel like redecorating."

"I figured you would."

Evan smiled. "Does that matter right now?"

"No, I don't think it does. Come here."

"Brat."

Harvey blushed as he wrapped his arms around Evan's shoulders, feeling the strands of Evan's beard tickle his chin. He smelled the floral powder and immediately withdrew, sneezing violently and nearly falling backward.

Evan cackled as he grabbed Harvey's hands to keep Harvey from tipping over.

"I'm *so* sorry," he said with a chuckle. "I almost forgot. Let me wash my face."

"Take your time."

"Won't you come with me?"

Harvey grinned, desire written all over his features. He trotted up the stairs after Evan, his lips quivering as his body began to tingle with anticipation. A wave of memories washed over him as he rounded the banister at the top of the stairs and padded his way down the hall into the main bedroom.

Nearly every piece of furniture was in the same exact place he had left it. The bed was positioned against the far wall, nestled between a pair of windows and two bedside tables. Lamps rested on each table as well as picture frames filled with smiling faces and landscapes. The silk sheets on the bed were undisturbed, having likely been made earlier in the day. On the left side of the room sat a cherry wood dresser, directly positioned across from the bathroom door.

Light flooded the carpet. Harvey followed the light with his eyes to the bathroom, listening to the familiar notes of Evan humming. He swallowed hard as he relaxed into the mattress.

Now that I'm here, I'm actually thinking about it, he reflected as he waited patiently for Evan to return. If I think too much, I might bail.

As if hearing his thoughts, Evan appeared in the doorway. His coat had disappeared, and a few buttons had been undone on his flannel shirt. Harvey rose instantly, crossing the room to aid in the removal of Evan's clothing. His fingers drifted down Evan's chest, Evan's stomach, and beneath Evan's navel. He tangled his fingers into the trail of hair leading to the waistband of Evan's jeans, tugging at the fabric hiding Evan's budding erection.

Evan sighed. He slipped his fingers into Harvey's hair, gripping a chunk as he often did in the past whenever Harvey initiated. He nudged Harvey back toward the bed with his hips and teased Harvey's lips with his bottom lip. As he continued to sigh against

Harvey's mouth, his hands expertly removed the barriers preventing him from exploring Harvey's body.

When Harvey collapsed against the bed, he took Evan with him. He whimpered as Evan searched between their writhing bodies for his twitching cock, gripping his shaft with cool fingers. He hissed as Evan's palm drifted up his shaft and down to the base of his cock to rest. His heart thumped rapidly as he parted his thighs, welcoming every possible move that Evan might make.

Evan pressed his shaft against Harvey's shaft, prompting a shuddering moan. He smirked crookedly as he nudged his nose into Harvey's neck and sampled the warm skin waiting for him to taste. Goosebumps greeted his lips and encouraged him to continue, his fingers dancing up and down Harvey's shaft.

Harvey twisted with every graze. He shivered as he wiggled his hips, his brows furrowing together in near concern as he struggled with whether to provide or receive pleasure. Although he knew what to do—considering he had slept with Evan for multiple years in the past—he was struck for the moment, almost frozen by the possibilities unfolding with each passing second.

As he arched his back, he allowed his eyelids to flutter. He gave his body permission to react to every touch, kiss, and whisper. He opened up to Evan and bucked against Evan's hard cock, practically panting as Evan swept lovingly over his shaft. He stole a glance to Evan's hand grazing over his cock and smiled wide, struggling to keep his eyes open and his brain focused.

He couldn't think. He could hardly get a word out in between moans. Everything that Evan was doing to him was making him weak and powerless. But he adored that very fact, savoring the tingle growing in his stomach that threatened to consume him. Evan sat up and flipped him over with a hungry growl, cupping his bottom lovingly. He arched his back and offered himself to Evan while parting his legs.

Evan drove his arm beneath Harvey's torso, gripping Harvey's right shoulder as he pressed his fingers against Harvey's entrance. His fingers outlined Harvey's entrance and coated it with saliva. Harvey bucked back, unable to control his hips. He leaned against Evan's cock with every intention of taking it, his breathing rolling in ragged waves as he felt Evan apply pressure.

When Evan slid inside, Harvey gasped. He threw his head back against Evan's shoulder and exhaled shakily, gripping Evan's hand that clasped his shoulder. Evan scooted his legs together and reared back, returning with eager pumps that deepened with each dive.

Each thrust conjured shivers from Harvey, currents of unruly bliss shooting through every limb of his body. He huffed as Evan hoisted him up and slid an arm beneath his waist. He was pinned close to Evan's torso—and he loved every second of it. As each piercing thrust became greedier, his stomach grew taut with anticipation. He wanted to burst.

And he wanted Evan to do the same.

He strained to turn his head, to find Evan's lips. He strove to express his pleasure through every moan-coated kiss, his lips quivering as his groans shifted to labored huffs. He felt Evan shift a hand to his exposed throat and whimpered louder as he felt Evan's fingers dance around his neck.

Though Evan never applied pressure, the presence of his fingers was enough for Harvey to tip over the edge of bliss into pure ecstasy. Harvey panted harder as Evan's fingers traveled up to his mouth, curious fingers slipping between his quivering lips. His eyes rolled back as he fought to contain his eruption.

But Evan's right hand had sank down to grip Harvey's cock, turning Harvey's effort of containment into a disaster. Just a few short pumps caused him to burst all over the sheets as Evan's invasion doubled in strength. Within seconds, Evan followed after Harvey and growled in Harvey's ear as he came.

Harvey collapsed against the bed, taking Evan with him. He crawled up the sheets and rolled to his side, shaking his head as he numbly reached out to grab Evan. His fingers and toes tingled as he shivered while tugging Evan into a lazy hug.

Evan huffed and whispered, "That...is something I definitely missed."

"You're telling me."

"I see it's been a minute for you."

Harvey chuckled lightly between gasps for air. "And for you."

"I couldn't help it. Moving on after you was..."

"Almost unfair."

Evan sniffled as he focused his gaze on Harvey. "Something like that."

"I felt the same."

"I'm sorry I avoided you."

Harvey shook his head. "Don't be. Let's just...enjoy the moment, okay? I want to enjoy this."

"I can do that..."

* * *

Harvey plucked a few pages from the printer and whistled as he walked back to his cubicle. He paused at Leo's cubicle, smiling as he set the printed pages to the right of Leo's mouse. Leo glanced up with a confused grin, speaking in a professional tone into the microphone of his headset.

While continuing to whistle, Harvey returned to his desk and plopped into his chair, maneuvering the mouse across the computer screen. He clicked on his emails and began working through them diligently. When his phone rang, he lifted his headset and shifted it over his ears, answering the call in a cheerful tone.

After handling the customer over the phone, he returned to work, typing rapidly on the keyboard. The keys clicked with every tap and filled his cubicle with the sound of productivity.

Leo popped up over the cubicle divider.

"Harvey," he said suspiciously. "Are you running a fever?"

"Nope. I feel great today."

"Oh?"

Harvey chuckled lightly, breaking his gaze with his computer monitor to gaze at Leo without breaking his typing stride.

"Yeah," he said. "You know I don't get sick."

"I know that, but you're usually not this chipper."

"It's really nice outside."

Leo squinted. "Are you on medication?"

"No, why do you ask?"

"Well, you're just..."

Harvey shrugged. "What? Happy? A guy can't be happy?"

"You got laid, didn't you?"

Harvey turned his eyes back to the computer monitor while trying to stifle a bashful grin. When he finished typing up his email, he sent it, then exited the email screen and turned slowly to Leo.

"Maybe," he replied. "But I'm not giving you any details."

"You met someone!"

"Leo, hush! Not so loud. Geesh, I don't want the whole office to know about my love life."

Leo clapped his hands as quietly as possible. "I can't believe it. You're seeing someone. Who is he? Tell me about him!"

"Maybe later. I have some work to do."

"Wow, you never pass up a chance to skip out on work."

Harvey shrugged with a slight grin. "Well, I'm feeling productive today. I want to make sure everything is done so my weekend is free."

"I can't imagine that's because you want to spend all your time volunteering."

"If it means I get to see this guy, then yes, technically."

Leo gasped dramatically. "Harvey, you *have* to tell me about him. Seriously, I can hold my calls."

"Patience, young Leo."

"Don't you sass me. I have a right as your best friend to know. We've been volunteering at the same place and I've only seen a handful of guys. Who is it?"

Harvey laughed while shaking his head. "You wouldn't believe me if I told you who I was seeing."

"Come on, Harv. It's not like you're seeing your ex-husband or something."

The silence that fell between Harvey and his best friend was palpable. Beyond the curtain of silence were the usual sounds of the office—soft voices speaking professionally, phones chiming, and keys clacking rhythmically. After a moment, Leo's eyes widened and he craned his neck over the divider.

"Harv, *no.*"

Harvey took a deep breath and gestured widely. "Well..."

"You can't be serious."

"I mean..."

Leo laughed suddenly, jogging around the divider to kneel in front of Harvey. He took Harvey's hands and squeezed them. "Spill. Now."

"I don't know what's happening," Harvey admitted in a low voice. "But we kissed over the weekend."

"Yeah? And?"

"*And* it led to other things."

Leo shook his head. His expression was unreadable, but the glimmer in his eyes told Harvey that he was intensely curious to hear more.

"I wouldn't read too much into it," Harvey explained. "It's probably because neither of us have been laid in a while."

"Sure, if that helps you sleep at night."

"Don't be like that. You know how I feel about my ex-husband."

Leo gave Harvey an appraising stare. "I'm not so sure I know anymore."

"Yeah, well, I guess that makes two of us."

"Harvey, how did that happen? I thought you wanted to avoid him at all costs."

Harvey shrugged. "I ended up becoming his elf."

"Oh, so it's a kink thing."

He laughed and playfully pushed Leo's arm, shaking his head as he leaned back in his desk chair. "You're ridiculous. It's *nothing* of the sort. It's just...I don't know. I guess we missed each other."

"Just be careful, okay? Rekindling an old romance can be nice and everything, but the problems of the past are waiting just around the corner. And as I recall, you two had *huge* problems."

"It'll be fine. It's nothing serious."

Leo stood up and planted his hands on his hips. "I'm going to worry regardless."

"You do that."

Leo chuckled and retreated to his desk. When he was gone, Harvey sighed and slid his cell phone from his pocket. He noticed a few texts from Evan. As he read them, his smile grew and he bit his lower lip.

"Do you want to come by the house on Wednesday and help me organize some of the winter events?" Evan asked. "I'll make dinner and hot cocoa."

"I would love that," Harvey replied. "What time?"

"You can come over whenever you're done with work."

Harvey nodded even though Evan couldn't see him. "I can't wait."

He set down his phone as his heart skipped a beat. Though he was convinced it wasn't serious, he couldn't help the giddiness that crept into his chest as he thought about seeing Evan again.

He simply couldn't wait.

Chapter Seven

Evan

The doorbell rang, shaking Evan right down to his core. He raced to the foyer and paused in front of the mirror near the door, running his fingers repeatedly through his hair. When he felt his appearance was sufficient, he opened the door with a wide smile.

"Harvey," he sighed. "You look great."

"I look like a penguin."

Evan laughed. "Well, that coat *is* big on you."

"I can't help that I'm always cold."

Evan nodded for Harvey to come inside. As Harvey unzipped his coat, he glanced around, intently studying the foyer. His eyes were round and bright as he observed the mirror hanging on the wall to his right and then the table sitting against the wall to his left. He walked to the table and rested his hand upon the wood.

After a moment, he turned to whisper, "It's weird being here."

"I know. I figured it would...Well, I figured we could talk about it."

"Right now?"

Evan shrugged. "Whenever you want."

"Maybe. I'm not sure yet. I wouldn't know where to start."

"How about we start by taking your coat off?"

Harvey smiled faintly. "I can do that."

Evan helped Harvey out of the oversized coat and hung it up on the coat hanger to the right of the door. He shut the front door, cutting off the cold breeze that threatened to chill him down to his bones. A shiver trickled up his spine and he huffed slightly as he led Harvey down the hall beneath the stairs to the living room.

A set of carpeted steps led down into the sunken living room with a couch positioned directly across from a fireplace. The left corner of the living room boasted a mounted television, and the right corner hosted a set of bookshelves overwhelmed with video games, gaming consoles, and various game paraphernalia.

Evan observed Harvey's slow tour of the living room.

"I see you painted the mantel," Harvey commented. "And you spruced up the fireplace."

"I fixed the broken bricks."

"It looks nice."

Evan smiled warmly. "Thank you. Should we get a fire going?"

"Sure, I'd like that."

"And what would you like for dinner?"

Harvey shrugged. "I'm not picky."

"That's a joke, right?"

"I'm not picky *anymore*. What do you want?"

Evan chuckled lightly. "Actually, I was hoping you could decide."

"I suppose we could order something."

"That's probably for the best. I didn't prepare anything."

Harvey rolled his eyes and smirked playfully. "What else is new?"

"I've been busy working on a new game," Evan explained as he whipped out his phone. "The company wants us to have testing finished by next weekend. And the game is...*phew*."

"What's the game?"

"It's a survival horror game."

Harvey arched his left eyebrow. "And you're working on this for Christmas?"

"We were supposed to release it for Halloween, but the development fell behind. We'll be lucky to have it done before the new year."

"Well, I wish you all the luck in the world."

Evan erupted with a throaty chuckle while scrolling through food options on his phone.

"I know you find video games boring," he stated. "But it's my passion. It's what I love doing."

"I know."

"So, we have Chinese takeout, Korean barbecue, American diner, and lots of other places available. We have tons of choices."

Harvey laughed as he drew up to Evan's side, leaning close to look over the choices listed on the phone screen.

"Choices are what killed us," he recounted. "But I'm feeling like having pizza. What about pizza?"

"Chicken, bacon, and cheese?"

"That's the one."

Evan smirked. "Can I add spinach?"

"To half the pizza. It better not touch my cheese."

"You got it, mister."

Harvey collapsed into the couch with a grin. He crossed his arms and folded his legs beneath him until he noticed Evan's stern glance. He rolled his eyes as he dropped his legs and kicked off his sneakers. He resumed his position and shrugged.

"I forgot. So, sue me."

Evan chuckled. "You're such a brat."

"Hey, I'm *not* a brat."

"If you're not, then you wouldn't like this."

Evan took Harvey's chin gently but firmly, drawing as close as he could without their lips touching. As he traced Harvey's lower lip with his tongue, Harvey shuddered and whimpered incoherently.

Evan pulled away with a knowing grin. "Told you."

"Shut *up*, Evan, and come back."

Harvey sat up on his knees and fumbled to grab Evan's shirt, gripping the buttoned fabric to tug Evan back to his quivering lips. He kissed Evan fiercely with bated breath.

Evan caught his shoulders and whispered, "Did you miss me?"

"A bit."

"I don't remember the last time we kissed this much."

Harvey smiled weakly. "It was a long time ago."

"Well, we can keep kissing as soon as I put in this order."

"All right, I'll try to behave."

Evan winked. "Good boy."

Harvey blushed as Evan sat next to him. Evan ordered their pizza and set his phone down on the coffee table, scooting it aside to reveal the empty fireplace. He jokingly smacked his forehead.

"The fire."

Harvey grabbed his collar. "Forget the fire. Come back and kiss me."

Evan dove willingly and happily to take Harvey's lips, sighing contentedly as Harvey returned the kiss. He sighed when he felt Harvey's hand slip under his flannel shirt. As Harvey explored his chest hair, he snaked his arm around Harvey's waist to deepen their kiss.

After a few minutes of passionate affection, Evan drew away, blinking lazily to clear his vision. Harvey seemed to reflect the same drunken lust, his lips twitching with desire as his eyelids fluttered. Evan chuckled as he stroked Harvey's cheek.

"Yeah," he sighed. "It's been a long time."

"What changed us, Evan?"

"A lot of things. Do you want to talk about it?"

Harvey hummed as he adjusted his position, tugging his legs underneath him as he sat facing

Evan. His eyes darted over Evan's shoulder, searching for something to focus on.

He shrugged. "I don't know."

"We can do that another day."

"Aren't we supposed to be organizing the events for the festival?"

Evan hissed as if he had been caught with his hand in the cookie jar. He shrugged and smiled sheepishly. "Oops."

"You just wanted me to come over, huh?"

"Yeah, I kind of did."

"Well, you didn't have to lie about it."

Evan smirked. "I'm sorry."

"And I'm sorry I wasn't brave enough to ask."

"But you're here now."

Harvey grinned. "Yeah, I am. I'm ready for that fire now. Do you want help with it?"

"Sure. Can you get the wood from the porch?"

"Yes, sir."

Evan huffed with amusement as he went to the fireplace to get the starter firewood. He heard the porch door slide open, cringing at the squeak of the door on the track as he balanced a few small pieces of wood inside the fireplace. He grabbed the candle lighter from the top of the mantel and held the buttons down, applying the miniature flame to the starter wood.

When Harvey returned, he piled the fresh pieces of cool wood on the starter wood. He stepped back and collided with the coffee table, tumbling backward.

Evan caught him before he could collapse and stood him upright.

"Careful," Evan warned. "There's a table there."

"I forgot."

"Apparently."

Harvey chuckled. "I was also distracted."

"How is it you could be distracted after hating me for three years?"

Harvey went silent as his brows knitted together. His eyes became glossy as the flames came to life, firelight dancing in his pupils as they darted repeatedly between Evan's eyes.

"I didn't hate you," he whispered shakily. "I was just angry."

"I was angry, too."

"It seemed like you didn't care when I left."

Evan sniffled, emotions overwhelming his gut as he guided Harvey to the couch. He invited Harvey to relax next to him, wrapping a comforting arm around Harvey's shoulders to tug Harvey close.

"I cared so much."

Harvey shuddered. "I did, too. What happened to us?"

"I guess we just had a difference of opinion."

"I'm sorry, Evan."

Evan frowned. "For what?"

"For everything."

"I'm sorry, too."

Harvey sat up, his eyes shimmering with tears waiting to trickle down his face. He sniffled and shook his head, fixing his lips with a knowing grin.

"Whatever," he said. "Let's just move forward."

"No talk needed?"

"We kind of talked."

Evan chuckled. "I guess we did."

"So, what have I missed over the past three years? How's everything been going?"

"All I've been doing is developing and testing video games. And volunteering. You know how I do."

Harvey huffed slightly. "Yeah, I do."

"What about you?"

"I guess it's just been work. I got a speeding ticket that I was ignoring for a while."

Evan laughed. "Speeding, huh?"

"I can't help it. I like a little exhilaration in my life."

"You were probably late for work."

Harvey attempted to hide his grin, but failed utterly, breaking into a guttural laugh that inspired Evan to do the same.

"Yeah, I was late," he admitted. "That's pretty on par for me."

"I know from personal experience."

"How is your family? Your friends?"

Evan shrugged. "They're all good. My parents keep treating me like I'm delicate, but I'm fine."

"Are you?"

"I swear, I'm fine."

Harvey nodded. "Well, that's good."

"How's your family?"

"They're a whole lot as they usually are. My brothers' wives have all popped out more babies. It's getting crowded during the holidays."

Evan chuckled. "June is about to give birth. She's been sharing the ultrasounds with me."

"When is she due?"

"Christmas, if you can believe it."

Harvey raised his eyebrows. "That's certainly a gift."

"I'll say."

"Do you still want kids?"

Evan frowned briefly, biting his lower lip, and lowering his gaze to Harvey's hands. He took Harvey's hands, squeezing them gently as he tried to huff away his anxiety.

"Maybe we shouldn't talk about that."

Harvey shrugged. "Suit yourself."

"Although I am excited for June. She promised I could visit after she gives birth."

"I bet that will be nice for you."

Evan shrugged. "Don't try to hide your disappointment. I know that was a point of tension between us."

"Well, that's in the past. I'm not worried about it."

"Really? Are you serious?"

Harvey nodded. "More than serious."

Evan grinned. He bit down on the anxiety swelling into his chest like the tide climbing up the shore in the evening. As he cleared his throat, he struggled to retain his grin.

He's lying, he thought. I can tell by the way his upper lip is twitching. He's going to pass it off as allergies if I say something, but I know him too well.

He eventually nodded, bringing Harvey's hands to his lips. Though the gesture was genuine, he felt dishonest with his internal dialogue. Still, he pressed on. He resolved himself to enjoying the evening—food and company alike.

And when the time came for Harvey to leave, he found himself wanting Harvey to stay.

Chapter Eight

Harvey

"Sorry, we have to make a pit stop," Harvey said while maneuvering the steering wheel. "I can't believe I'm late again, Jesus."

"Sorry, my name is Evan."

Harvey cackled. "Listen, I know this is last minute, but I *promised* my parents I would stop by before the festival."

"Your parents?"

"Yeah, they...Ugh, my brother is in town and he wants me to see my nephews."

Harvey studied Evan out of his peripheral vision, noticing the slight nod that Evan gave. He caught the worried expression before Evan had time to fix it. When he paused at a stoplight, he turned fully to Evan with a warm smile.

"This isn't a *meet-the-parents* thing, okay? It's just a timetable issue. We have to set up the cabin again later, so I figured we would do this all with one car."

Evan smiled and huffed with amusement. "It's okay. I already know your parents."

"I know you know."

"And I know that you know that I know."

Harvey chuckled lightly, turning to observe the light. "You're ridiculous."

"How about you just admit that you like being around me?"

"I will do *no* such thing."

Evan snickered. "You will by the end of the night. Just you wait."

"You'll have to torture it out of me."

"Oh, I have my ways."

Harvey rolled his eyes as the light turned green. He let his foot off the brake and gently pushed on the gas pedal, following the afternoon traffic toward his parents' neighborhood street.

"I'm sure you do," he teased. "But you wouldn't dare employ those methods while I'm driving."

"And how do you know that?"

"Because I know that you—"

Evan traced the back of Harvey's neck, causing Harvey to shiver. His eyelids fluttered as he slowed the vehicle down, preparing to make a right-hand turn on Florence Ave. When he reached the driveway of his parents' house, he stopped the car, put it in park, and turned to grab Evan's face.

He kissed Evan as if they hadn't seen each other in centuries. He slipped his fingers into Evan's hair, stroked Evan's scalp, and then dropped his hands to Evan's shoulders. As he drew slowly away, he felt electricity crackle between their lips. His eyelids drooped. He could hardly keep them open.

"Wow," Evan whispered. "I guess I should have prepared for retaliation."

"I guess so."

"So…"

Harvey blinked lazily and smirked. "So?"

"You like being around me, don't you?"

"It's not the end of the night, Evan."

Evan chuckled and shook his head while sitting back in the passenger seat. He didn't say anything. He simply watched as Harvey maneuvered the car into the driveway and shut it off.

Harvey jingled the keys in his right hand. "In and out. Fifteen minutes."

"You keep telling yourself that, but I'm positive that your mother will kidnap me when she sees me."

"I sure hope not. We can't have the festival without Santa."

Evan laughed while exiting the vehicle. Harvey followed suit and led the way up the porch steps, his heart fluttering in his chest as he approached the front door.

I haven't told my parents that Evan and I are talking now, he thought as he raised a shaky hand to knock. If she says anything about it, I swear I'll—

The door wheezed open and revealed a short woman wearing a forest green dress with a white apron over it. Her hands were covered in flour and her hair seemed to match, most of the dark brown strands now streaked with silver and white.

She gasped, "Evan?!"

"Oh, right. Your son stands right here, but say hi to *Evan*."

She disregarded her son and yanked Evan into the house, pulling him into a warm embrace. "I haven't seen you in years!"

"It certainly has been a while, Eloise. I see you've gotten prettier."

"Oh, stop it. Come in! I'm making muffins for the kids. You should meet them. Oh, they're getting so big!"

She grabbed his hand and jerked him in the direction of the kitchen, leaving Harvey on the doorstep with a dumbfounded expression. Harvey sighed as he took a step into the foyer and shut the door behind him. Just as he began shedding his coat, he heard the sound of sneakers stomping against the wooden floor.

Two small boys came barreling down the hall followed by a rather tall and far more muscular version of Harvey. Harvey knelt down to greet his nephews.

"Baxter! Travis! You're so big!" he exclaimed.

"Hey, brother," his brother said. "You're late."

"Yep, that's me. Always late. How are things going, Adam?"

"Great! I just got a raise at the firm. It's been going beautifully."

Harvey forced a smile as he stood up. "That's wonderful."

"What about you? How's that insurance gig?"

"It's not a gig. It's a job."

Adam laughed. "Same thing."

"Where did Evan go? Did our mother steal him?"

"Yeah, she took him to the kitchen. Listen, if you're ever tired of the money you make, you just let me know. I have connections."

Harvey forced another smile, bordering on a grimace. "I'll certainly keep that in mind. Let me go find Evan."

"Who's Evan?" Travis asked while grabbing Harvey's hand. "Uncle Harvey, who is your friend?"

"Uh, he's just a friend," Harvey replied while walking to the kitchen. "Gosh, you've gotten tall. How old are you now?"

"I'm almost four."

"Incredible."

Adam spoke behind him, but he ignored it in favor of sitting at the kitchen table. His mother had already roped Evan into helping prepare the muffins. She was talking rapidly—as she often did on too much coffee or too much excitement—and shooting partially confused glances at Harvey.

Harvey drummed his fingers against the table, offering reassuring smiles at Evan whenever Evan glanced in his direction. After his mother sidled away from the table to grab the baking sheets, Evan leaned over to Harvey and whispered, "This is weird. Why is she being so nice?"

"She always loved you," Harvey whispered in return. "Just embrace it. Five more minutes."

"You just have to wait until they're baked," Eloise insisted while setting the baking trays on the table. "Santa needs his treats before he goes to work."

"How do you know I'm Santa this year?" Evan asked. "I mean, aside from Harvey telling you."

"He didn't tell me squat. I saw it in the festival email. You always did it every year when you two were married."

Harvey blushed and sank down in his seat. "Well, I mean, *duh*."

"You're right. I did," Evan agreed with a gentle grin. "I guess I can't help it. It's my favorite time of year."

"And we're so thankful you're here. Harvey is such a grump around the holidays."

Harvey closed his eyes briefly and exhaled, "*Mother*."

"It's true. Isn't that right, Adam?"

Adam smiled and nodded from the doorway leading into the living room to the right of the kitchen. The boys had gone back to playing, making a medley of sounds that resembled dinosaurs or feral animals. Adam bounced from the doorway and patted Evan on the back.

"Do you want to meet the boys? Travis is three and Baxter is one. I don't think you had the pleasure of meeting them yet."

Evan beamed. "I would love to meet them."

As Harvey began to protest, his mother set a baking tray in front of him and scooted the bowl of muffin mix toward him. She gave him a knowing grin as she sank into the chair to his left.

"So," she said in a low voice. "What's going on with you and Evan?"

"Nothing is going on, Mother."

"Well, he kept looking at you."

He chuckled nervously. "That's because he wasn't sure why you were being so nice to him."

"That's because I love him."

"That's what I told him."

She snickered and started setting multicolor baking cups into the muffin tray. She traded trays with her son and pointed to the bowl, indicating for him to start pouring the batter.

Harvey reluctantly obeyed. He sighed as he filled each baking cup with the same care and precision as his mother had taught him. After a moment of silence, he set down the bowl and studied his mother.

"What do you think is going on?"

She shrugged. "I didn't say anything about that."

"But you *think* something is going on."

"Harvey, I *thought* you two got a divorce. Then, you show up with him three years later. What am I supposed to think?"

He blinked rapidly, unable to regain the smile he had been wearing when he had walked into the house. Although his features were smooth, he could feel a confused grimace surfacing, the sort of annoyed expression that he wore whenever he was dealing with a particularly testy customer.

"I don't know what's happening," he admitted. "We've been hanging out because I volunteered for the festival."

She squared her gaze on him. "You volunteered? *Voluntarily*?"

"Well, it's for a ticket."

"See, I thought so."

He huffed with amusement. "But it's been nice spending my time there. I'm enjoying it."

"Is that because it's enjoyable or because Evan is there?"

"I can't keep anything from you, can I?"

She smirked. "I'm your mother. I know everything."

"We're just working together for now. We have to hit the festival after this, so I thought I would bring him along to save time and gas."

"Well, next time you do that, let me know. I'll make something for you both to take so you don't have to sit around waiting."

He shook his head. "Mother, I don't mind waiting. It's just—"

"It's just you can't stand your brother."

"It's not that, Mother."

She eyed him carefully, her gaze sharply inquisitive. He fell silent as soon as her gaze fell upon him, stunned by the authority in her features.

"That look," he joked after a moment. "It's your *look*."

"It's how I get things done."

"You always gave Adam and me that look when we were rolling around in the mud."

She laughed as her eyes sparkled with the memory. "You two tracked so much mud into the house that I had to mop *twice*."

"But you still loved us."

"Yes, I did. And I still do, even if you two don't exactly get along."

He shook his head. "Adam and I are just...different kinds of people. He's high up in the business world while I'm content where I'm at."

"I always thought you were more suited to a smaller family, Harvey, but then again, I love that you're part of this family. You're my son. And even if you can't get along with your brothers, I'll still love you."

"Oh, come on, Mother. Don't get sappy."

She giggled. "It's the holidays. I'm allowed to get sappy."

Harvey rolled his eyes.

"All right, get to it," she commanded. "That batter isn't going to pour itself."

"Yes, Mother."

As Harvey finished pouring the batter into the baking cups, he listened to Evan playing with the boys in the living room. The sound invited him to stand, to nearly abandon his task. He quickly poured the rest of the batter and went to the living room where he found Adam sitting with a newspaper on the recliner near the television.

Evan sat in the middle of the floor with both boys and a mess of dinosaurs scattered in every direction. A few train cars sat upright while others sat on their sides, and Baxter, the younger of the two, was bouncing between the tracks they had set up and the volcano near Adam's feet.

Wow, he's a natural, Harvey reflected as he watched Evan play with his nephews. *He seems like he's enjoying it, too.*

"And what's this one?" Evan asked curiously.

His voice was void of the usual high-pitched tone that most adults put on when they spoke to children. He seemed genuinely curious, and he expressed it every time he asked the kids a question.

After some time, Harvey sighed and walked over to Evan, tapping Evan on the shoulder.

"We have to get going," he said. "We're going to be late."

"And we can't have that, can we?" Adam snipped from the other side of his newspaper. "Fifteen minutes. Like always."

Harvey glared at his brother as Evan stood up from the floor. Evan shot him a concerned expression to which he shook his head. He fixed a grin on his lips and nodded toward the door before turning to his nephews with a bright expression.

"I'll see you guys later, okay?"

He knelt down and embraced his nephews despite their cries of opposition. As he assured them he would return, he backed away toward the door, reaching for Evan's hand. It might have been out of habit or out of need, but Evan didn't seem to mind.

And Harvey didn't mind either.

Chapter Nine

Evan

The winter festival was in full swing by the time Evan had led his parade of elves and helpers to the grand red chair in front of Santa's cabin. When he relaxed into the chair, he extended his arms, inviting the first pair of children to his chair.

Harvey jumped into action, guiding the pair of kids up to Evan. Each child sat on one of Evan's knees and he spoke to them in a low, kind voice, asking them what they would like for Christmas.

"A rocking horse," the girl replied. "And I want everyone to be happy."

"Well, I want a water gun," the boy added. "I want to have one for my sister, too."

"Those are all wonderful things to ask for," Evan said. "You must remember to be good. And not just for Christmas, but for the whole year. Remember, Santa always knows."

He added a wink for effect and then turned to the elf working the camera.

"Smile for Santa!" the elf instructed.

The children beamed as a flash of light illuminated their faces. Evan patted them on the back as they hopped down and wished them a Merry Christmas. When Harvey brought a new pair of children, Evan repeated the process: asking them what they wanted for Christmas and reminding them to be good. He must have met fifty children by the time the elves announced it was time for Santa to take a quick break.

Harvey took his place on Evan's right, resting his hand on Evan's shoulder and leaning toward Evan's ear to whisper, "You were a natural with my nephews today."

Evan grinned and gestured around. "I've had practice."

"Of course, but I think it also comes naturally for you."

"Thank you for not making it a big deal."

Harvey grinned as he stood upright. "Well, I *might* have enjoyed watching you play with them."

"Do you mean that?"

"Santa!" a little girl shouted. "Santa, don't forget me!"

Evan perked up when he heard the little girl's voice and grinned wide when a blonde-haired child about six-years-old darted beneath the red ropes to race to his chair. He opened his arms when he recognized the girl.

"Marissa!"

"Hi, Santa!"

He stood up to embrace her, lifting her up and causing her to giggle.

"Santa is on a quick break, sweetie," Harvey said. "Can you wait a few more minutes?"

"Oh, I have plenty of time for this one," Evan insisted. "Where's your father? Is he around?"

"He's back there."

Marissa pointed to the man standing awkwardly beyond the red ropes. The man raised a hand in greeting.

Evan grinned. "Matthew, come over here!"

Matthew shrugged and then chuckled as he jogged past the ropes, embracing Evan as soon as he was close enough to do so. When he stepped back, his daughter joined his side.

"We're sorry we missed you last year," he said. "Marissa had the flu."

"But I'm all better this year!" Marissa exclaimed.

"And I'm so glad that you are," Evan stated with a grin. "What would you like for Christmas, dear?"

"Can we get a picture?"

"Yes, of course!"

He plopped down into his chair and invited Marissa into his lap. As she whispered in his ear, he smiled and nodded, listening intently to everything she was listing—which seemed to never end.

"Can you get someone for my Daddy?" she requested. "He's been so sad lately. I think if he had someone to love, he would be happy."

Evan grinned warmly. "That is such a sweet thing to ask for, Marissa. I'll see if I can work some Christmas magic."

She giggled. "Thank you, Santa."

"All right, smile for the camera!"

After the photographer snapped a picture, Marissa bounced from his lap and went back to her father. He stood up to embrace Matthew again.

"Your daughter is still so sweet," he expressed once she was out of ear shot. "Are you doing all right?"

"Oh, it's been a little lonelier than usual, but I'll be fine."

"Well, you have my number. Let me know if you need anything."

Matthew nodded with a grin. "Thanks, Evan. I mean, *Santa*. I'll see you around."

"Merry Christmas, Matthew."

When Matthew and his daughter had drifted away, Evan returned to his chair. He noticed Harvey looking intently at him.

"Something wrong?" Evan inquired.

"Who was that?"

Evan shrugged lightly. "That was my ex, Matthew. We had a brief relationship after you and I got a divorce."

"Does he visit you often?"

"No, this is the first time I've seen him in a while. Why do you ask?"

Harvey shook his head, chuckling lightly. "No reason. I was just...curious."

"Harvey, are you jealous?"

"Me? Jealous? That's silly. You know I don't get jealous. I just get—"

Evan grinned knowingly. "Insecure."

Harvey raised his eyebrows, appearing to be surprised by Evan's response. He fumbled with the bell at the end of his hat, causing it to jingle slightly as he twisted and turned it.

"If you twist that any harder, you're going to break the bell right off," Evan teased. "Are you okay?"

"Was I doing that? Sorry, I didn't mean to."

"Harvey, take a breath. Nothing is going on between Matthew and me."

Harvey gave a small grin. "I didn't think that but thank you for saying so."

"Of course."

"Do you want to come to my apartment after this? I can make us hot chocolate since your pseudo wife isn't here."

Evan chuckled. "I would love that, Harvey."

* * *

As Harvey unlocked his apartment door, Evan waited patiently behind him, studying the oversized coat that nearly swallowed his neck. He struggled with the door and cursed under his breath, inspiring Evan to intervene.

"Hey, I've got it," Evan offered.

"I've got it."

"No, you don't."

Harvey huffed with frustration. "Evan, you're doing that thing."

"What thing?"

"You're not letting me do it myself."

Evan frowned while stepping back. He held up his hands as a sign of surrender. "Sorry."

"I appreciate that you want to help, but I said I've got it."

"You're right."

Harvey turned the key with strained effort, then pressed his shoulder against the door to get it to open. He smiled victoriously as he allowed Evan entry into the living room.

"See?"

Evan snorted, a playful grin taking over his lips. "I see. You're a big, strong man."

"Don't sass me."

"Then, I'll do something else instead."

Harvey shut the door and bolted it, hanging his keys on the hook to the right of the door. "Like what?"

"Turn around and find out."

Evan watched as Harvey shed the fluffy coat. After hanging it up, Harvey turned around and met his mouth with a sigh of desire. He was delighted to find that Harvey was receptive to their dueling lips. He guided Harvey to the couch, stumbling slightly as he fought to loosen his torso from his coat. As he fumbled with the buttons of his flannel shirt, Harvey's cool hands slid beneath the fabric, causing him to whimper and shiver.

He shoved Harvey on the couch and whipped away his shirt, revealing a torso decorated with reddish-orange hair. Harvey eagerly coated his chest with loving hands that darted in every direction possible. He nestled between Harvey's legs, unable to stop kissing Harvey's soft lips. He reached between them and cupped the front of Harvey's jeans, eliciting a desirous moan from Harvey's mouth.

He sighed as he surfaced to meet Harvey's gaze, whispering, "Can I go down on you?"

"Yes, please..."

Evan grinned as he sank south. He unbuttoned Harvey's jeans and tore open the zipper, hungrily procuring Harvey's cock from its hiding place. He traced Harvey's soft shaft with his parted lips and exhaled over the head of Harvey's cock. As Harvey's cock twitched to life and grew hard, he swallowed the tip and slowly sucked Harvey's length into his mouth.

Harvey tangled his fingers into Evan's hair. He thrust his hips eagerly, skin erupting with goosebumps as Evan touched every visible surface. With every slurp and suck, he throbbed, his fingers curling harder into Evan's hair and encouraging Evan to do much more than merely suck.

When Evan surfaced, he rose to greet Harvey's lips and worked Harvey's jeans away from his hips. He repositioned himself between Harvey's legs and rubbed his swollen cock against Harvey's, returning every groan that emerged.

He spat into his hand and circled Harvey's entrance, then spat again to add more lubricant to his cock. While pressing the tip of his cock to Harvey's hole, he felt Harvey buck and smirked at the movement. His eyelids fluttered as he pressed his forehead to Harvey's forehead and waited for an invitation.

Harvey smirked while grabbing Evan's hips. He pulled Evan inside, gasping and arching his back to accept Evan's throbbing cock. He exposed his throat as he snaked his hand to the back of Evan's neck, inviting Evan to sample his naked skin.

Evan gladly dove into Harvey's neck. He rhythmically pumped to fill Harvey's hole, trembling with every withdrawal. As he doubled his piercing pumps, Harvey squirmed beneath him, prompting him to part Harvey's legs wider. He raised Harvey's knees and pinned them to the cushions of the couch to provide him more room to thrust.

A primal urge to let loose surfaced within him, rising into his chest, and expanding throughout his body. The desire propelled him as he sat up to crown Harvey's bottom with his hips. He tossed his head back and sighed as he drifted perpetually in and out of Harvey. As Harvey tightened around him, he slowed his thrusts, opening his eyes and focusing on the sweet man beneath him.

"Are you all right?" he asked while leaning toward Harvey's lips.

"I'm fine," Harvey whimpered. "It just feels..."

"What?"

"It feels so *good*."

Evan grinned triumphantly, picking up speed when Harvey gripped his hips again. He searched for Harvey's cock, gripping Harvey's shaft loosely as he rhythmically stroked. He watched Harvey's features shift—pure delight, utter terror, uncontrollable bliss, and pleasurable torture washed over Harvey's face in quick succession.

There was no one expression that could have incited Evan to act more than when Harvey was in the throes of passion. He quickened his pace, matching his thrusting hips to his stroking hand. His gut twisted as he nudged deeper, fervent thrusts erupting with every nudge of Harvey's hands.

Soon Evan's movements became a flash, matching his desire to erupt. He stroked Harvey generously as he thrust feverishly to meet their mutual explosion. As the valve withholding his orgasm snapped, he unleashed himself inside Harvey, watching with satisfaction as Harvey erupted as well.

He fell in a victorious heap on top of Harvey, sweating profusely and panting erratically. Harvey reflected much the same reaction, dragging his fingers up and down Evan's back. He lazily kissed Evan's neck and then patted Evan's back to indicate he wanted to get up.

"Do you need anything?" Harvey struggled to ask as he huffed his way to the kitchen. "Water?"

"Yes, water."

Evan relaxed into the cushions of the couch with a worried expression.

We usually cuddle, he thought. But he got up right away this time.

When Harvey returned with two water bottles, Evan fixed his expression, smiling gratefully at Harvey as he accepted a water bottle. He took a quick sip and set it on the coffee table while Harvey relaxed into the couch next to him.

He glanced expectantly at Harvey. "Do you want me to stay?"

His heart skipped a beat when he noticed Harvey's expression wavering. But soon, a smile erupted on Harvey's lips.

Harvey whispered, "Yes, please stay."

"I can do that."

Chapter Ten

Harvey

Harvey returned to his apartment on Tuesday afternoon with a grin and a box of baked goodies from his job. He set the box on the table near the kitchen and shed his winter coat, hanging it near the front door. He wandered up to the coffee table in front of the couch and stared at the cushions where, just a few days prior, he and Evan had danced into fits of pure pleasure.

The smile on his lips widened.

I still can't believe this is happening, he thought. He frowned suddenly as he recalled the festival on Saturday. And I still can't believe his ex-boyfriend showed up. I bet Evan loved the fact that his ex had a daughter.

He rolled his eyes as he flipped around and tossed himself on the couch. He did his best to relax, forcing his muscles to loosen as he studied the television across from him. He observed his reflection in the black screen and noticed that his frown hadn't dissipated.

What am I supposed to do with all this time off? It's not like I want to see my family.

He cleared his throat as he sat up, propping his elbows on his knees, and dropping his gaze to the cable box sitting on the entertainment center just beneath the television.

I could binge a show, read some books, or call Evan.

He smirked.

I'll call Evan.

But as he reached for his phone, a pang of unease shot through his gut. He whipped his phone out despite the feeling and opened his text message thread with Evan. Throughout the day, they had sent silly pictures and jokes to each other. All seemed to be well in the world of Harvey and Evan, and yet Harvey's questionable discomfort swelled.

He sighed as he sat his phone on the coffee table. He rose resolutely from the couch and wandered into the kitchen, preparing a pot of coffee for the afternoon. His fingers lingered on the handle of the carafe as the machine bubbled to life. Soon, the heavenly aroma of coffee filled the apartment.

He pursed his lips as his thoughts continued spinning in his brain.

I remember when we fought over having kids. It was around this time. He wanted to surprise me with a surrogate.

He shook his head as he searched the cabinet to his right for a mug. He set the mug next to the coffee pot and waited eagerly for the pot to finish filling. Unable to wait, he snatched the carafe from its place and poured the hot liquid into his mug.

I was livid. I couldn't believe he went behind my back and spoke to a woman about impregnation. And how had he planned on doing that? By donating our sperm. How strange.

He shook his head as he added powdered creamer and a scoop of sugar to his coffee. He stirred the liquid generously, watching the shade shift from black to caramel brown. As he raised the mug to his lips, he closed his eyes, inhaling the wonderful scent of roasted coffee beans. He took a quick sip and smiled, opening his eyes again.

But things are different now, right? I mean, we're rekindling our passion. He's receptive to me. He's trying to be respectful. He backed off when I told him not to help me.

He hummed as he watched the rest of the carafe fill with coffee. While studying the dark liquid, he squinted and shrugged his shoulders, trying to shake away the discomfort he felt while recalling holiday memories with Evan.

The holidays were never my favorite. He knew that. Why in the world would he bring up such a topic around a time that I despise?

After a sigh, he carried his coffee back to the living room where he noticed the notification light on his phone blinking red. He lifted his phone, unlocked it, and discovered a text from Evan.

It read, "Do you want to go for a walk tomorrow in the park by the ocean? We could grab that hot chocolate we skipped on Saturday."

Harvey sniffed with amusement as he relaxed into the couch. He took another sip of his coffee before setting it down, handling his phone with both hands. His thumbs hovered over the digital keyboard.

Though he wanted to walk with Evan, his heart was telling him otherwise.

What do I say? It's not like I'm doing anything else. I don't want to be around my family and I don't want to be alone.

His dilemma grew when another text arrived from Evan, saying, "You could come over and help me with some decorations."

Harvey shook his head.

Every argument began with us decorating. We would spend hours in a fight while trying to make the living room appear cheerful. It was awful. I don't want to repeat that.

"I think a walk would be great," he typed before he could change his mind. "Decorating, not so much."

"Still a grump about Christmas, huh?"

"You should know."

Evan sent a laughing emoji and added, "I'm just teasing you, Harv. I can pick you up tomorrow."

"What are you doing tonight?"

"Do you miss me that much?"

Harvey rolled his eyes to the ceiling as a mischievous smirk played over his lips. He focused on his phone again and responded, "Maybe."

"I'm busy tonight with some leftover game development. Otherwise, I would love to have you over."

"I can be quiet."

"You know I can't concentrate when you're around."

Then, why are we even hanging out?

Harvey furrowed his brows as he typed, "I guess that's a blessing and a curse."

"We always were able to be present for each other. Let's be easy about it this time around."

"This time?"

Evan sent a heart emoji. "I think I like where we're going this time."

"Really?"

"I mean, yeah. We seem to communicate a little better."

Harvey huffed slightly, a smile lingering on his lips. "I guess time will tell us more. You're lucky I even want to see you so close to Christmas."

"I'll take it as a gift from the universe."

"I didn't think you still liked me this much. It makes me feel weird."

"Is it too much?"

Harvey rested his phone on the coffee table. Though his spirits had been lifted since he had started seeing Evan again, he could hear the alarms blaring in the back of his brain.

It is too much. And I don't know how to express that.

He lifted his phone and typed, "Everything is fine. I'll see you tomorrow, okay?"

"Are you sure?"

"I'm absolutely sure. Don't worry yourself sick, Evan."

"As long as you're sure. I'll see you tomorrow."

After Harvey set down his phone, he reached for his coffee and took a few quick sips. The liquid had cooled enough to avoid burning his upper lip. As he took a greater gulp, he shrugged his shoulders to get the weird sensation out of his body.

But no matter how much he moved or shrugged, he couldn't rid himself of the worry that they were retracing heavily trodden paths from the past.

What do I do? How do I cope with this?

He shook his head and grabbed his coffee, walking to the patio door. He slid it open and stepped into the cool afternoon, leaving the door open behind him as he sank into one of the patio chairs. He studied the apartment complex around him, absorbing the sight of Christmas lights, garlands, and various other decorations that his neighbors annoyingly saw fit to hang up.

He slurped his coffee as he sat quietly. He listened to the city erupt around—the hum of traffic whooshing past the complex, dogs barking in the distance, and children giggling on the nearby playground. His ears perked up when he heard two men talking below. His eyes dropped to find them and located them in the parking lot just beneath his balcony.

When he tore away his gaze, he glanced at the building sitting across from him. The neighbor directly positioned across from his patio had green and red lights strung around the wooden gate guarding their patio. The lights blinked rhythmically even though it was relatively early in the afternoon.

He shook his head.

I haven't done any decorating. I haven't even gotten a tree. What's the point? I hate Christmas.

He sighed while setting his coffee mug on the table to his right. He folded his hands in his lap and continued observing the world around him. Something in the air had changed.

And it wasn't the weather.

It's me, he reflected. Something about me has changed. And it has something to do with Evan.

Chapter Eleven

Evan

Evan squinted at the horizon as he strolled lazily along the cement path. To his left, Harvey wandered at the same pace, appearing to be occupied with something other than the statues adorning the park. He studied the lines etched into Harvey's forehead, the eyebrows knit tightly above Harvey's nose, and the lips firmly drawn in a tight line above Harvey's chin.

"Something wrong?" he whispered curiously. "You look worried."

Harvey perked up. His expression shifted, revealing a cool calm. "Just cold."

"Again?"

"Hey, you know me."

Evan chuckled lightly. "I do."

"And you're a human heater. Why don't you share some of that?"

"Do you want me to wrap my arm around you?"

Harvey laughed. "Duh."

Evan obediently slipped his arm around Harvey's shoulders. He smiled as Harvey nestled close, Harvey's hand hooking to the top of his zipper. Harvey played with the zipper idly.

"June is getting ready to burst," Evan said. "I'm so excited."

"Yeah, it must be exciting."

"I can't wait to see her baby. I think she might ask me to be the godfather."

Harvey nodded slowly. "That sounds wonderful."

"I know you don't like kids, but maybe you could be a godfather, too."

"I haven't quite worked on my mob outfit just yet."

Evan cackled, pausing on the path to hold his gut. Harvey tugged him into a brief hug and then released him, inviting him to continue walking toward the edge of the park where the ocean met the shore.

"If you know I don't like kids," Harvey spoke carefully, "then, why would you say something like that?"

"I figured it would be a good compromise."

"I didn't realize that was something we were supposed to compromise on."

Evan took a step back while retaining Harvey's hand. He frowned slightly as the breeze swirled around them, causing Harvey's messy hair to flutter around his forehead.

"I just figured we could talk," he explained, "and maybe we could come to a sort of agreement."

"What kind of agreement?"

"Something we could both agree on."

Harvey let out a loud *pfft* and moved his hair out of his face. He kept his gaze on the ocean while blinking at the hair that didn't move out of his face.

"I don't know," he sighed. "What would that even look like?"

"What would you want it to look like?"

"Evan, I don't want kids. That's a firm stance."

Evan huffed slightly while releasing Harvey's hand. "It's just an idea."

"I don't get why you would bring it up. I didn't want kids three years ago and I don't want them now."

"I wasn't suggesting that we have kids, just that we live vicariously through someone else."

Harvey shook his head. "I already do that with my pesky brothers. They have enough kids to make me avoid reproducing for another four lifetimes."

"That's pretty harsh, Harvey."

"Well, that's what I am: Harsh Harvey."

Evan's frown deepened, the corners of his mouth digging into his jaw and prompting him to take another step away from Harvey. It was as if the energy radiating from Harvey was forcing him to put distance between them.

And Harvey noticed. He blinked rapidly as he asked, "Why are you looking at me like that?"

"I just don't understand why you're hanging out with me if you know I want kids."

"I guess I could ask you the same thing about me not wanting kids."

Evan shrugged lightly while turning toward the ocean. He watched the waves lap at the shore, studying the way the seaweed shuffled underneath the white foam. After taking a deep breath, he slipped his hands into his pockets.

"I don't know," he admitted. "I just wanted to talk about it."

"Well, I don't."

"I don't understand why you're being so hard about this."

Harvey chuckled, though he hardly seemed amused. "I don't understand why it's something you continue to bring up."

"Because it's part of what I want out of my life. And I want you in my life, so why wouldn't I try to find a solution that works for us both?"

"I don't see a solution to this, Evan."

Evan swallowed hard. "You're being impossible."

"No, I'm being *reasonable*. I've had enough experience with my nephews to know that having kids would be awful for me. I can't stand the sound of babies crying and I make an awful father figure."

"With that attitude, you sure do."

Harvey gaped at Evan. "See, that's why it wouldn't work."

"Because I'm agreeing with you? I don't see what's wrong with that."

"No, it's because you insist on pushing my boundaries. I don't want kids, Evan. That's it. End of story."

Evan shook his head. "Then, I guess this won't work. Again."

"You said that last time. How many times are you going to break up with me because of this?"

"I don't see *you* fighting for our relationship."

Harvey gestured vaguely around him. "What's worth fighting for here? You won't let the past go and you won't allow me to have a future without any children involved."

"I think you're the one who won't let go of the past. You keep harping on me about this."

"Because *you* keep harping on *me* about this."

Evan snorted with disdain. "I should have had June replace you the moment you walked into the cabin. I knew it was a bad idea."

"I guess hindsight is twenty-twenty, huh?"

"You're confirming it pretty well right now, Harv."

Harvey crossed his arms and shook his head. "And you're doing much the same. Is that all?"

"Actually, I think it was rotten of you to lead me on if you knew I wanted kids so badly. I think it was horrible that you kept seeking my company after realizing that I *still* want kids."

"That's not my fault. I thought you changed."

Evan huffed with defeat. "Yeah, I thought the same thing about you, sweetheart."

"Don't call me that."

"Well, it's better than the alternative."

Harvey arched his right eyebrow. "We're already fighting. Go for broke. Call me whatever your little heart desires."

"You wouldn't be able to handle it."

"You're doing it again. You're trying to determine what I can and can't handle. You're trying to do things for me. I *hate* it when you do that, Evan."

Evan shook his head. "Well, you're not very good at making decisions for yourself. How's that speeding ticket? Have you done enough community service to pay it off?"

"That's none of your business."

"You made it my business. And I'm willing to bet that you'll make the same mistake again."

Harvey laughed nervously. "All the more reason for me to avoid having children."

"Yeah, you could say that again."

Evan shoved his hands deeper into his pockets. As he stared at the waves crashing in front of him, his lower lip quivered and he felt a sob rising in his throat.

Not in front of Harvey, he begged silently. Don't break in front of Harvey. That's exactly what he wants.

He shook his head as he backed away from his ex-husband.

"I'm leaving. This is ridiculous."

Harvey waved. "Bye, Evan."

"You don't even care."

"I did care at one point, Evan. But then you made it a point to demonize me and use it to sabotage something beautiful. Think about that over the holidays."

Harvey flipped around on his heel, taking the opposite path to head back to the parking lot. Evan stared after Harvey with shock written all over his features, absorbing the last statement that Harvey had made.

He swallowed the sob attempting to rise from his throat all over again.

Am I sabotaging this? Does he really believe that?

He dropped his eyes to the cement path and studied the cracks, using the tip of his boot to trace them.

I don't think I should believe that for a second. Harvey is just pulling a Harvey. He's trying to get me to feel bad because he feels bad.

After a moment of silence, Evan turned around and briskly walked toward his car. He hopped inside and turned the key in the ignition, not bothering to wait for the engine to warm up before exiting the parking lot. He saw Harvey walking adjacent to the street leading to the park.

He pulled up next to Harvey and rolled down the passenger window.

"Harvey," he called out. "You can't walk home. It's cold."

"I'm fine!"

"Just let me drop you off."

Harvey turned his bewildered gaze to Evan, eyes burning with anger. "I don't want your help!"

The sight of Harvey's enraged features inspired Evan to roll the window up and take off without a second thought. He drove until he got home, sitting in the driveway for a while as he stared at the steering wheel. He hadn't yet shut off his car. He hadn't even turned on the heat. The cab was freezing, biting through his winter coat, and causing him to shudder uncontrollably.

His lips quivered as he focused on the garage door.

It's over. And I think it's over for good this time.

He shut off the engine and stepped out of his car, slamming the door shut behind him. When he got inside, he stripped away his coat and hung it up near the door, turning his blurry vision to the empty foyer.

"I still love him," he stated shakily. "How can I still love him when we can't agree on what we want?"

He shook his head as the sob he had desperately attempted to keep down broke from his throat. He stumbled toward the living room and dropped onto the couch, hugging one of the cushions to his face. As the air around him vibrated with sorrow, he continued crying into the pillow, unwilling to allow even his empty house to witness his frustration.

His tears soaked the pillow and caused the fabric to stick to his face. When he finally sat up, he sucked in great gulps of air, having been unable to breathe properly with his face shoved into a cushion. He shook his head as a few errant tears trickled down his cheeks.

After snorting to clear his nose and throat, he glanced at the fireplace sitting across from him. He noticed the charred brick, the stained hearth, and the metal pokers resting to the right. He dragged his eyes up to the mantel where a picture frame hosted a photograph of Harvey and him posing in front of a tree.

He darted across the room and snatched the picture from its place, taking it to the kitchen. He dumped the frame into the trash and marched to the staircase, taking the steps by two. When he reached his room, he collapsed into his bed, hoping that the grief would soon pass.

And when it didn't, he reluctantly fell asleep.

Chapter Twelve

Harvey

Christmas music floated through the air as Harvey settled on a stool at the bar, drooping over the counter like a branch weighed too heavily by snow. He waved with a practiced grin at the bartender, inviting the man to walk over to him.

"Hey, Harv. What would you like?" the bartender asked.

"Scotch on the rocks, Greg. Two, please."

"That bad, huh?"

Harvey chuckled. "Nah, Leo should be here in a few minutes."

"Ah, the double duo at it again. There's karaoke later if you guys want to stick around."

"I'll consider it."

Greg chuckled and prepared the drinks, setting them on the counter in front of Harvey. Harvey paid for the drinks, left a rather large tip, and then shooed the bartender away. He felt someone pat his back and looked up to find his best friend standing next to him.

He grinned weakly. "Hey, Leo."

"You doing all right? You have two drinks."

"One is for you. I'm not even that bad."

Leo chuckled and added, "Yet."

"Hey, I've got a handle on my drinking."

"You're certainly doing better than a few years ago."

Harvey shrugged while he lifted his drink and took a quick sip. As he set it down, he whispered, "Well, that was the year my husband left me."

"Are you sure you're feeling okay? You look pretty off."

"You know I hate the holidays."

Leo nodded. "I get it. I haven't seen my family in years."

"I'm sorry, buddy. I forgot they don't invite you anymore."

"Yeah, well..." Leo faded as he lifted his drink and downed the whole thing. He sighed as he relaxed into the stool next to Harvey and waved the bartender over for a refill. "I've got you."

"And that's why we're here."

"You ever think about moving out of the state and starting over?"

Harvey raised his eyebrows. "Are you thinking about moving?"

"No, but I've considered it before."

"I don't know. Maybe. I guess."

Leo chuckled lightly. "I just think that there's not much for me here. The gay scene is dull and boring. Nothing exciting happens. I don't know. Maybe I'm just feeling the winter blues."

"I can understand that."

"At least you have your family nearby."

Harvey snorted. "I don't necessarily like being around them. I wish they would get off my back."

"About what?"

"You know what."

Leo nodded slowly. "Yeah, when I did have my family around, they were pretty heavy on the pressure to reproduce."

"And I got it from Evan, too."

"Haven't you been seeing Evan lately? How's that going?"

Harvey downed his refill and waved for Greg to pour more into his glass. He watched the liquid slosh the ice cubes around, grinning when the glass was halfway filled.

"Thanks," he said while setting his card on the counter. "Can you open a tab?"

"Of course."

When Greg disappeared, he turned to Leo, saying, "It's went as well as anyone could have expected."

"Went? As in past tense?"

"Yep."

Leo frowned sympathetically. "Do you want to talk about it?"

"It's the same as it always was. He wants kids. I don't. End of story."

"I don't think that's the end of your story, Harvey."

Harvey shrugged with defeat. "Well, it is. And there's no way to change that. I don't want kids. I *never* have wanted kids. I don't see how we could compromise."

"What if you made a case to Evan about living without having kids?"

"Trust me, that doesn't work. I've tried."

Leo nodded. "What about you? Would you ever consider it in the future?"

"My position hasn't changed."

"Damn, that's a pretty big problem to be having."

Harvey blinked away the tears that threatened to fall. He sniffled to clear his sinuses and then coughed to clear his throat.

"It's whatever," he sighed. "I'll get over it."

"Well, I'm here for you."

"Thanks, Leo."

Harvey fell silent as he cradled his drink. He listened to the ice cubes clink around inside the glass and inhaled the scent that rose from the liquid. As he took another sip, the music in the background changed to a recent top-chart pop hit.

He smiled gratefully and raised his glass in Greg's direction.

"Thank God," he whispered. "I thought I was about to puke."

"Yeah, I like Christmas, but the music makes me want to gag."

"You're not missing much by not having family around here."

Leo shrugged. "Still, I think I could put up with a little music just to have them around."

"I'm sorry. I'm being insensitive."

"You're just a little tipsy. Want to grab a table?"

Harvey shook his head. "The bar works just fine."

"Do you want me to set you up with someone? I bet I could find a nice guy for you for the holidays."

"No, I just want Evan."

Leo gave Harvey an appraising glance. Harvey realized what he had said and tried to hide behind the sleeve of his sweater as his cheeks grew hot with embarrassment. He stumbled over an explanation. Syllables echoed from his lips, but hardly made any sense as he tried to string them together. He dropped his hand to the bar and shook his head while biting his lower lip.

"I can't believe I just blurted that out," he whispered. "I must be drunk, not tipsy."

"No, I think you're just hurt."

Harvey focused on Leo. "Of course, I'm hurt. Evan was my best friend. He was the love of my life and I've lost him forever because I can't have a decent conversation with him."

"I think if you two were to actually sit down, you could work around this whole 'having kids' thing."

"I don't know, Leo. It feels hopeless."

Leo shrugged. "I mean, it's Christmas. Anything can happen."

"I don't believe in that sort of thing."

"You don't have to. I'll believe in it for you."

Harvey turned a warm grin to his best friend, relief causing his shoulders to relax slightly. He adjusted his position on the stool and sat upright, lifting his glass from the counter.

"I don't know what I would do if I was alone in this."

"You'd probably drink yourself silly."

Harvey laughed. "You might be right."

"What do you think you're going to do? Obviously, you want Evan."

"Yeah, I guess I do."

Leo chuckled. "There's really not much guessing here, Harvey."

"I just wish I could make everything better without having to do all this hard work."

"This hard work is what makes a relationship. If Evan still loves you—which I'm willing to bet that he does—then, he'll be happy to sit down with you and talk things out."

Harvey shook his head. "I'm pretty sure I ruined it. I told him that he was sabotaging the whole relationship."

"Yikes."

"Yeah, I... I didn't mean to say that."

Leo shrugged. "You could call him and apologize, right?"

"I hate apologies."

"Well, that's part of a relationship, too."

Harvey sighed and shook his head. "It's the day before Christmas. He's probably busy with his family. And even if I did call him, he probably won't answer."

"You never know until you try."

"Why are you helping me so much with Evan?"

Leo cocked his head to the left. "You know, despite how you two ended, Evan made you happy."

"I don't know about that."

"You *do* know about that, Harv. I saw it in you every day you came to work. You were a huge bubble of joyful energy. When you two got a divorce, you caved and became rotten."

Harvey's eyes widened. "Ouch."

"I'm sorry. I know that's harsh, but it's true. When you started seeing Evan again, that spark of happiness returned."

"That's an interesting observation."

Leo nodded. "I think it's an important one to note. Despite your differences, the two of you love each other and want to be with each other."

"He did offer a compromise."

"And what was the compromise?"

Harvey took a sharp breath and held it as he drank down more of his scotch. He set the empty glass on the edge of the counter, subtly indicating to Greg that he wanted more. After the glass had been refilled, he held it loosely in his hand, using it to gesture around.

"He offered me to be a godfather to his friend's kid," he explained slowly, chewing carefully on each word before it left his mouth. "And honestly, I don't know if I would be good for that."

"Why not?"

"Have you met me? I'm not exactly the pinnacle of great decisions."

Leo laughed. "No, but you can change."

"Do you really think so?"

"Sure. I have all the faith in the world that you can change."

Harvey shook his head as his features sank. "I've never been too good at change."

"Hey, everybody has a hard time with something. For you, it's doing things differently, maybe even unconventionally. But if either of us have learned anything about having unconventional sexual preferences, it's how to roll with the punches."

"Yeah, I guess that's true."

Leo smirked. "You guess?"

"Okay, fine. I *know* that's true. I'm just having a hard time with it."

"And that's okay. Change doesn't happen overnight."

Harvey nodded. "It was nice seeing him play with my nephews. He's a natural with kids."

"Yeah?"

"Yeah, he..." Harvey coughed nervously. "He looked like he really enjoyed it. Maybe I can start there."

"Listen, you don't have to change your core beliefs to be with someone. You don't have to change your mind about having kids. That's your lifestyle decision and no one should dictate whether you keep it or not," Leo explained. "But compromise is worth it when you love someone. As long as it's reasonable compromise, the relationship can thrive."

"When did you get so smart about these things?"

Leo laughed. "Hey, I might not be able to keep a relationship for longer than six months, but at least I can make it a great relationship. I'm big on communication."

"That seems to be what it takes."

"It does. Even friendships require it."

Harvey smiled warmly. "I'm glad you're communicating with me."

"Well, you're my best friend. You're kind of stuck with me."

"Thankfully."

Harvey held out his glass and clinked it gently against Leo's. He shifted his weight on the stool and shrugged his shoulders to loosen the tight muscles between his shoulder blades. He sighed as he set his glass down on the counter.

"If I do this," he said slowly. "If I apologize, how should I do it?"

"I'd say go big or go home."

"What do you mean?"

Leo shrugged. "Show him you care with a huge gesture. This isn't a phone call kind of thing. Be extravagant. Be wild."

"So, set a few Christmas trees on fire?"

"Harvey!"

Harvey cackled. "I'm kidding, Leo! God, get with the program. I hate Christmas, remember? That would be right up my alley."

"Please, don't set anything on fire unless it's Evan's heart."

"I don't even know how to do that."

Leo patted Harvey's shoulder. "What's Evan's favorite thing to do?"

"He always liked those stupid sleigh rides they have in the park downtown."

"Yeah?"

Harvey perked up, raising his eyebrows high on his forehead. "I could probably set that up for tomorrow."

"That sounds like an expensive venture."

"If I go now, I can probably catch the guy and pay him."

Harvey stood abruptly from his stool, nearly knocking it over. He waved for Greg to walk over and paid for his tab, leaving a nice tip before snatching his receipt and card from the counter.

"How much do you need?" Leo asked while whipping out his wallet. "Actually, you know what? I'm coming with you."

"This is a one-man mission, Leo."

"No, it's a community mission. My best friend is getting his ex-husband back. We're doing it together."

Harvey smirked while Leo marched resolutely to the entrance of the bar. He paused at the door, turning expectantly to Harvey.

"Well, lover boy, let's go!"

Harvey laughed as he caught up to his best friend. His heart fluttered in his chest as he followed Leo to the park.

And though the air was chilly, he felt warmed by the flames of passion. He felt comforted by the strength of his determination. He felt fueled by the drinks in his system.

And most of all, he felt hope.

Chapter Thirteen

Evan

Evan sat in the recliner next to the fireplace as his parents divided the presents sitting under the tree. He wore a worried smile as he attempted to focus on the precious time he was spending with his family. His parents were sitting on the ground near the tree with dozens of boxes and bags sitting in between and around them.

"Glenn, did you really wrap this with shipping paper?" his mother asked jokingly as she held up a rather large box. "Or did you just shove it under the tree after it came in the mail?"

"Hey, brown wrapping paper is a classic," his father claimed. "Get with the times, Katelyn. This is how the kids do it now."

"Is that so?"

"That *is* so."

Katelyn turned her playful yet curious gaze to Evan who was hardly paying attention. He cradled a mug of hot cocoa in his brawny hands, running his thumbs along either side of the ceramic.

"Evan? Are you there?"

Evan glanced up like a child who had been caught with a cupcake after he had been told not to have one. He widened his smile, deepening the lines in his forehead and cheeks.

He cleared his throat and asked, "What's that, Mom?"

"I asked if the kids do brown paper for gifts these days."

He shrugged lightly. "Ah, I wouldn't know. I prefer the colorful stuff."

"See?" Katelyn teased as she turned to her husband. "Evan gets it."

"Why don't you just open it, dear?" Glenn suggested. "You'll see the inside is worth much more than the outside."

"I guess I'll just have to find out."

She tore away the paper, discarding it to the ground where paper had already begun to pile up. Evan witnessed his mother's surprised reaction to her gift: a brand new coffee machine that could also make espresso. Her entire face lit up with delight as she embraced her husband.

"Glenn, this is wonderful."

Glenn beamed. "I thought you would like it. You got something else to go with it, too."

He held up a glittering red bag that had a reindeer drawn on the side. She accepted the gift with a loving grin and then turned to Evan, raising her trim eyebrows in his direction.

"Evan, you haven't opened any of your presents."

Evan sighed shakily. "I'm just not in the spirit this year, Mom."

"Is it boy trouble?"

Glenn playfully elbowed Katelyn. "Kate, you can't just poke into people's personal business. Whatever is going on, Evan will share in his own time."

"He looks so sad." She turned to her son and repeated, "Evan, you look so sad. What's going on?"

"I'm just tired, Mom."

"It's more than that. You look upset."

Evan tried to smile, his lips quivering as he attempted to contain his emotions. He rose from the recliner and sighed as he wandered into the kitchen, walking to the stove to refill his mug of hot cocoa. When he had sufficiently refilled the mug, he returned to the living room and sat on the ground with his parents.

"I saw Harvey," he whispered. "At the festival."

"What happened? Did he bother you?"

He shook his head. "No, we...We actually started hanging out again."

Her eyes widened. "And you didn't tell us?"

"I was worried it wasn't going to last. And I was right about it."

She took his hand and squeezed it gently. "Oh, dear. You've got those winter *and* romance blues, huh?"

"Well, he never was a particularly nice guy," Glenn pointed out. "He was pretty rude to you the last time he was here."

"I think that might have been my fault," Evan admitted.

"Hardly," Glenn argued. "Even if you had done something wrong, that's no excuse to treat someone that way."

"Dad, it's not that. It's the pressure I was putting on him to start a family."

"Oh, I remember this," Katelyn recalled. "You two couldn't agree on having kids. Is that still the same now?"

Evan nodded glumly, staring into his mug. "Yep."

"Well, your father and I had the same thing happen, but here we are. We're still married."

Evan stared at his mother. "Wait, you guys disagreed on having kids? When?"

"Before you, obviously," she replied with a chuckle. "But we decided to have you. It was sort of an accident, really."

"When we met, I wanted to start a family immediately," Glenn explained. "Katelyn was resistant to the idea of having kids. She was so firm about it that I almost left."

"Almost," she emphasized.

"But we ended up talking it out and left things open-ended."

Evan shook his head. "But how? How the hell did you two do that?"

"We talked," she replied while shooting a grin in the direction of her husband. "We talked for a *very* long time. And we didn't rush into anything either."

Glenn nodded, returning the grin. "The moment I respected your mother's decision was the moment we were able to compromise."

Evan studied his parents, observing the love that floated between them. He recalled this look from his teenage years. Despite what happened in or around their family, they always seemed to look at each other with the same affectionate gaze. A smile spread across his lips as he continued to study them.

"I see," he whispered. "That's interesting."

"So, are you two done for good?" she asked.

"I don't know. I guess so. We had a pretty bad argument."

She nodded with understanding emanating from her eyes. "Hey, arguments happen. That just means there's an opportunity to talk later. You never know what might happen."

"God, I think I owe him an apology."

"I'm sure the time will come for that."

He chuckled. "How can you be so sure?"

"Because it's the season for that magical stuff. It's just part of the holidays, you know?"

Glenn laughed. "Your mother is a hopeless romantic."

"Hey, I like to think love wins at the end of the day. Isn't that right, Evan?"

Evan grinned. "I like to think so, too."

"So, how about you open some of your gifts? I'm sure that will make you feel better, even if it's just for five minutes."

"I think I can manage that."

She plucked a small box from the ground near her feet that was wrapped with shimmering green foil and a red ribbon. Evan smiled as he accepted the box. He pried the ribbon away and dropped it to the ground, working away the green wrapping next. He revealed a velvet black box with a circular silver design stamped on the top.

"I know you're not much for material things," she explained. "But I figured this would be something nice to wear for New Year's."

Evan popped open the box to find a silver watch nestled in black silk. He procured the watch reverently and held it up to the light, watching the surface reflect the multicolored string lights blinking on the tree behind him. He smiled at his mother and father.

"Thank you," he whispered.

"Do you want me to help you put it on?"

Glenn chuckled. "Katelyn, let him do it himself. He's thirty years old."

"Sorry, I'm just excited."

Evan huffed with amusement. "I see where I get it from."

"What are you talking about?"

"Nothing, Mom. I love it. I'm putting it on right now."

She smiled as Evan fastened the watch to his wrist, holding it up to show it off to his parents. As he studied the chain design of the band and the polished face of the clock, he heard his phone buzz from across the room. He stood to locate it while his parents chatted in the background.

When he found his phone, he noticed he had received a few texts from June. He clicked on them and smiled uncontrollably as he looked through the pictures June had sent from the hospital room.

"June had her baby!" he announced while running to his parents. "Look! She named the baby Serenity. What a beautiful name."

"Oh, look at that little baby!" Katelyn cried while snatching the phone. "She's so tiny. How much does she weigh? Is she okay? She looks jaundiced."

"Mom, she was *just* born like an hour ago. She's not going to be chunky right off the bat."

"I hope she grows into a chunky baby. Those are always the cutest babies."

Glenn and Evan shared a laugh. Evan shook his head as his mother continued to spout off her preferences for babies—what they should wear, what they should be fed, and how they should be raised. He relaxed into the recliner and smiled at his parents who were fawning over the pictures that June had sent.

I wish I could tell Harvey, he thought somberly. I wish I could show him the pictures. I wish he were here right now.

He closed his eyes for a moment while focusing on the memory of their argument at the park.

I said some things I regret. And I can't take them back. Why did I let my anger get the best of me?

He perked up when his mother scooted over the floor to hand him his phone. He smiled weakly, holding the screen up to his face so he could look at June's messages again.

"I want you to be the godfather," she had written. "And I think having a matching godfather would be pretty swell, too."

Evan allowed his smile to warm his features as he typed, "I think that would be wonderful, June."

"So, how about it?"

"I fully accept my role as godfather."

"Anyone else to add to that role?"

His thumbs hovered over the screen, shuddering slightly as he tried to formulate a response. After a pause, he texted, "I think I have someone in mind, but I'm not sure how he feels about it."

"Just let me know. We're glad to have you as part of our family and anyone else you deem fit."

"I'm glad to be part of your family."

When he sent the text, he stared at the screen for a long time. He considered texting Harvey but thought better of it as he realized he had already asked Harvey about being a godfather. And as he glowered in the sullen energy that his thoughts provoked, he received a new text message.

This time, it was from Harvey.

His eyes widened as he clicked on the notification.

"Meet me at the park later," it read. "I have something for you."

I can't believe it. Has he gone mad? Am I hallucinating?

Evan stood abruptly from the recliner and paced toward the kitchen, rounding the corner to walk into the hallway leading to the foyer. He stood in front of the door as he studied the screen, blinking repeatedly to clear his vision.

No, it's there, he thought as his heart skipped a beat. Harvey texted me. He wants to meet later.

"When?" he wrote. "What time?"

"7:00 PM. And don't be late, mister."

Evan chuckled while shaking his head. "I've got a new watch that will keep me from being late."

"Good. This is important."

"What is this about? What are you doing?"

"What I should have done a long time ago."

With a sigh of relief, Evan held his phone to his chest. He closed his eyes and allowed the relief to fill every crevice of his body, inviting him to relax every muscle that had tightened since his argument with Harvey. He returned to the living room wearing a love-drunk expression that his mother immediately pointed out.

"What happened?" she pressed. "Is it the baby?"

"It's Harvey," he replied. "I think something magical is about to happen."

Chapter Fourteen

Harvey

Harvey stood next to the sleigh as the wind bit his cheek. He squinted against the unforgiving breeze, watching the horses tied to the sleigh whinny and fill the air with puffs of white condensation. He glanced up at the man sitting at the front of the sleigh. The man held the reins loosely, his top hat and suit appearing to be from another era.

"Just a few more minutes," Harvey said. "I'm so sorry, Winston."

"Don't worry about it, Harvey. I'm sure he'll come along."

"Yeah, it's just strange. Evan is never late to anything."

Winston chuckled lightly. "Have a little faith."

"I'm trying."

Harvey shuddered as the breeze doubled down, causing him to hug his shoulders and whistle. Gusts of white condensation huffed from his trembling lips, reminding him exactly how cold it had gotten. When he glanced at the sky, he noticed the pockets of amorphous black between the fluffy gray clouds. A few droplets of rain landed on his nose which seemed to thicken the air with a foreboding chill.

He shook his head. "All right, I'm calling it."

"Just a second, Harvey," Winston advised. "I think I see someone."

Harvey squinted at the dark figure approaching. He cracked a grin as he recognized Evan. The sight of Evan both put him at ease and made him nauseous, reminding him of the lengthy speech he had prepared.

He took a shaky breath and raised his right hand in greeting.

"Evan, hey," he spewed quickly. "Hey, I'm glad you came. I'm sorry I didn't call. I mean, I figured you were busy with your family, and I didn't want to bug you, and I know you've been waiting on June, and—"

"Harvey," Evan intercepted. "Relax. Take a breath. Your lips are blue."

"Oh, I..." Harvey chuckled as he dropped his gaze to Evan's boots. He couldn't quite make eye contact. But he didn't exactly want to look away. As he forced himself to meet Evan's gaze, his shoulders relaxed and some of his shivering subsided. He smiled and whispered, "Thank you."

"Of course."

"So, what do you think?"

Evan regarded Winston with a jolly grin. "Hello, Winston."

"Good to see you, Santa."

"Has business been booming?"

Winston nodded. "Ever since the first of the month."

"That's good to hear."

"Are you two ready for a ride?"

Evan turned his warm gaze to Harvey, practically melting Harvey on the spot. Harvey bit his lower lip and gestured to the seat on the back of the sleigh.

"After you."

"Thank you, sir."

Harvey took Evan's hand, helping Evan up into the sleigh. When Evan was seated, he followed suit, resting on the bench next to Evan. He tapped his fingers against the wood between them nervously as the sleigh jolted forward, the sound of hooves clopping against the cement echoing off the nearby buildings.

"So, how do you know Winston?" Harvey asked while folding his fingers together in his lap. "I mean, other than the fact that you know everyone in Charleston."

"We had sleigh rides at the festival, remember? Winston would bring Smoke and Thunder along to give rides to the kids."

"Ah, I guess I missed that detail."

Evan grinned jovially. "That's okay. You weren't around the festival a whole lot back then."

"I wasn't around for much at all, really."

"Well, that's in the past."

Harvey shook his head. "Evan, about that..."

"You don't have to explain yourself."

"No, I do. I need to apologize for that. I'm sorry I didn't pay much attention to you. I was running because I didn't know what to do. I didn't know how to handle our disagreement."

Evan nodded slowly, his gaze falling to the space between them. "I understand that. I think I did the same thing."

"Yours is justified. It was a response to my actions."

"I think I played as big a part as you in us parting ways, Harvey. Let me apologize, too."

Harvey hesitated, studying Evan's serious features. He started to reach for Evan's beard, but thought better of it, retracting his hand and dropping it back into his lap.

"I shouldn't have pressured you the way that I did," Evan continued. "I should have sat down with you and talked about it instead of assuming it was the end of us."

"I should have done the same thing."

"But saying what we should or shouldn't have done won't change what actually happened."

Harvey nodded glumly. "I know. I can't fix it."

"You're right. You can't fix it."

"What?"

Harvey stared at Evan for a few minutes with a mixture of fear and confusion, watching a smile grow on Evan's lips.

"But *we* can," Evan whispered.

"What are you saying?"

Evan grinned as he met Harvey's gaze. "I don't need to have children with you to have a fulfilling life with you."

"But Evan, you've always wanted kids. I've been getting in the way of that. I've been preventing you from that happiness."

"No, you haven't prevented me from achieving anything. I've prevented it myself by limiting my perspective with you."

Harvey shook his head. "Don't sacrifice what you want for me. Don't do that."

"Weren't you just about to do the same?"

"No, I... I was going to try..." Harvey licked his lips nervously before continuing, "I was going to suggest a compromise."

"Harsh Harvey wants to compromise? Are you drunk?"

Harvey laughed. "Hardly."

Evan glanced at his shiny watch. "Well, it's still early. We could always grab drinks later."

"You want to grab a drink with me?"

"Or we can have one at my house. Or we can have one at your apartment. We can have one wherever you like."

Harvey grinned shyly, daring to reach for Evan's hand. "I'm sorry I accused you of sabotaging us. It wasn't right to say that. I was hurt and angry. I was confused. I was worried about us going right back to the past."

"We practically did."

"But then I started thinking that maybe there was a point to that. Maybe we were supposed to have that argument."

Evan furrowed his brows together with concerned curiosity. "Why would that need to happen?"

"I love you, Evan. And I would do just about anything to be with you. But I won't sacrifice pieces of myself just to be with you. I think I needed to realize that."

"I feel the same way."

Harvey smiled warmly. "Which is why I was thinking that—if it was still an option like you said—I would consider being a godfather to June's baby."

"Are you serious?"

"Yes, I've given it plenty of thought. And I think, well, if the baby isn't around all the time, then I won't make a ton of mistakes around it, right? I mean, I can practice how to act around a baby. I can try to change some behavior. I can cut down my drinking and—"

"Harvey?"

Harvey froze, settling his gaze on Evan. "Yeah?"

"Shut up and kiss me."

Harvey whimpered as he fell into Evan, accepting the kiss Evan was passionately delivering. His heart lurched in his chest as his hands searched to cup Evan's face, tangling his fingers into the strands of Evan's beard. He sat comfortably in this position for a few minutes while the air around them crackled with energy.

When he drew back from the kiss, he noticed a few flakes of snow sitting on Evan's head. He studied the crystal flakes with heated interest until he noticed the flurry of snow dancing around the sleigh. He gasped as he gripped Evan's shoulders.

"Evan, it's snowing—I can't believe it!"

Evan turned to observe their surroundings, his features a reflection of joy and wonder. Snow decorated his beard and melted almost instantaneously, only to be replaced by more that fell from the sky. Harvey tipped his head back and opened his mouth to catch a few flakes on his tongue. He giggled like a small child and wrapped his arms around Evan, burying his cold nose into Evan's warm scarf.

"This is a miracle," he whispered. "I can't believe it."

"I can. It's magic."

"There's no such thing."

Evan pulled back from their embrace while holding Harvey's shoulders, his eyes sparkling with delight as he insisted, "Yes, there is. It brought us back together."

"Communication did that."

"Call it what you want, but I think it's magic."

Harvey smirked. "I suppose we can blame Christmas for that, huh?"

"Hey, I thought you were a Christmas grump."

"Maybe being around you has softened me to the idea that Christmas isn't really that bad."

Evan grinned. "I'm glad I could do that for you."

"You know, my best friend reminded me of something."

"What's that?"

Harvey took a deep breath and sighed it out. "We were happy once. Before we ever worried about having kids or not, we were deeply in love. I want to get back to that. I think we can."

"I don't think it takes that much work to get back to that, Harvey. I'm willing to sit with you. I'm willing to leave things open-ended."

"Really? You would do that?"

Evan nodded. "My parents actually had disagreed once on whether they should have kids. My mother never wanted any but my father did. She told me how they compromised."

"Wow, I guess if they hadn't had kids, I would never have met you."

"That's true."

Harvey stroked Evan's cheek. "I just want us to be together without worrying about anything else. I want to make good memories with you. I want to change."

"Harvey, you don't have to change anything about you."

"Yes, I do. I want to change my attitude. I felt rotten without you. I felt like I couldn't tackle the day. Now, I feel different. I feel like I could handle more if I just tried."

Evan smiled warmly. "I want you to take your time and do what you need to do. I don't ever want to force you to do anything or to try to take over when you're trying to do things yourself."

"Thank you, Evan."

"I mean it. I'm not meddling in your business."

Harvey arched his right eyebrow. "So, no interfering when I'm struggling with the front door, right?"

"You won't have to worry about that anymore."

"Why's that? Are you going to fix my front door?"

Evan smirked. "No. I want you to move back in with me."

Harvey's eyes widened. Tears danced at the edge of his vision as his smile stretched uncontrollably across his face. The corners of his mouth seemed to poke into his eyes, causing them to brighten as he looked at Evan.

"Are you...Are you sure about that?"

Evan nodded. "I'm positive. When you came over, I realized how much my house—*our* house—felt empty without you."

"Oh, Evan..."

"I've been trying to find the missing piece for years. I've been trying to fill that house with video games, collectibles, and even other people. But none of them worked."

Harvey's lower lip quivered as he whimpered, "I feel the same."

"But when you were there, I felt complete. I felt warm. I felt *right*."

"I would love to move back in."

Evan blinked, prompting a couple of tears to trickle down his left cheek. He sniffled as Harvey swept his tears away.

"Maybe we can do that before the new year," he suggested. "What do you say?"

"That's a lot of moving to do in less than a week."

"All right, how about the end of January?"

Harvey grinned. "That sounds doable to me."

"And I think I have another idea as far as a compromise."

"What's that?"

Evan winked. "You'll have to forgive me because it's a late Christmas gift."

"Evan, what is it?"

"I can't tell you. It's a surprise."

Harvey laughed as he struggled to exclaim, "Evan!"

"Hey, you can wait! I promise it'll be worth your while."

"I'll do my best."

Evan grinned while wrapping Harvey in a hug. He rubbed Harvey's back and chuckled lightly, alerting Harvey of his happiness.

"Thank you for the sleigh ride," Evan whispered. "This means so much to me."

"Well, I wanted to show you that I was serious."

"I believe it."

Harvey smiled as he drew back to look into Evan's eyes. "I'm glad you do. I believe you. And I forgive you."

"I forgive you, too."

"I love you, Evan."

Evan smiled wide, running his thumb over Harvey's cheek. "I love you, too."

Harvey dove for another kiss. He didn't mind the jolt of the carriage as it careened through downtown. He didn't care about the people laughing and dancing on the sidewalk to their right. All he cared about was Evan and how he was going to spend his life with Evan.

When he drew back from the kiss, he rested his head on Evan's shoulder and tugged Evan's arm around his shoulders. The rotten feeling in his gut that he had carried for years melted away, chased into the sun by Evan's brilliant love. As the horses drew them back to the park, he sat up and squeezed Evan's hand.

"How about that drink?" he asked. "My house or your house?"

"How about *our* house?"

Harvey grinned. "I can do that."

Chapter Fifteen

The fire crackled rhythmically in the fireplace as Evan set down a plate of freshly baked chocolate chip cookies on the coffee table. He returned to the kitchen to grab two tall glasses of milk, setting them on either side of the plate. When he heard the sound of Harvey's soft footfalls descending the stairs, he fixed his sweater, smoothed his right hand through his hair, and put on his best smile.

"Good morning," he greeted when Harvey appeared. "How did you sleep?"

"Better than ever. Are those...Are those cookies?"

"I figured we could have them for breakfast."

Harvey chuckled as he sleepily shuffled up to Evan and planted a kiss on Evan's cheek. Evan beamed.

"And if cookies don't work?" Harvey asked.

"Then, I'll make something else."

"Well, let's not be *too* hasty about the cookies not working."

Evan chuckled. "Can I give you your gift now?"

"I had almost forgotten about gifts."

"That's what happens when you spend two days in bed with your ex-husband."

Harvey giggled and lifted a cookie from the plate. He tapped his bottom lip with it as an idea flashed across his eyes.

He focused on Evan as he said, "I've been thinking about that."

"What about it?"

"What if we weren't divorced anymore?"

Evan cocked his head curiously to the left. "Are you sure about that? We just got together."

"You might be right. It could be too soon."

"Oh, I don't know. We still have the new year to look forward to."

Harvey squinted playfully. "What are you trying to say?"

"I'm saying there might be more than one gift under that tree for you."

"Well, bring them over."

Evan laughed as he relaxed into the couch next to Harvey. He wrapped his arm around Harvey's shoulders, burying his face into Harvey's neck. He inhaled the scent of Harvey's cologne that was tinted with hints of oak and sighed as his eyelids fluttered.

"I want to cuddle first," he said. "Can we cuddle?"

"I don't think we've ever touched this much before."

"There's always room for change, right?"

Harvey chuckled. "You made such a big deal out of gifts a couple of days ago and now you're stalling."

"Maybe I'm just waiting for the right moment."

"All right, while you're *stalling*, how about you tell me about June's baby?"

Evan sat upright and snatched his phone from the table. He opened the newest pictures of Serenity and held the phone up for Harvey to see.

"Wow, that's...She's so small!" Harvey exclaimed while grabbing the phone from Evan. "How do they even make them that small?"

"Have you ever met an infant?"

"Well, when my brothers had their babies, I didn't meet them for a few months. They were bigger by then, I assume."

Evan laughed. "Serenity is only a couple of days old."

"So, she had her baby on Christmas? That's adorable."

"I think it's sweet. We can go meet her if you want."

Harvey smiled weakly as he bit into his cookie. He munched on the cookie for a while, staring at the fire dancing in the fireplace. The morning light illuminated his features and filled his eyes with reflection.

He hummed curiously. "Do you think I'd be okay holding a baby?"

"Well, you don't have to hold her if you don't want to."

"Yeah, that might be best."

Evan chuckled. "You'll be fine, Harvey. June would love for you to be Serenity's godfather."

"I still need to spruce up my mob suit."

"You're such a *dork*."

Harvey laughed, dropping the uneaten half of his cookie back on the plate. He wrapped his arms around Evan and pulled Evan into him, sighing contentedly as Evan rubbed his back.

While buried in Harvey's t-shirt, Evan smiled wide. He listened to Harvey's heartbeat and nuzzled as close as he could get, shivering when he felt Harvey scratch his scalp. His mouth slacked as his eyes closed.

"You're going to put me to sleep," he said as he quickly sat up. "I can't fall asleep now."

"Why not? It's still early. It's a Sunday. There's no reason we can't nap on and off throughout the day."

But then we would miss picking up your gift, Evan thought with a grin. And I don't want to miss that.

"What?" Harvey asked. "What are you staring at?"

"Just you."

"That's weird."

Evan laughed. "Then, I'm a weird guy. I don't mind that label at all if it means I get to keep staring at you."

"I'm hungry for more than cookies. What have we got in the fridge?"

"I can make a full breakfast."

Harvey grinned. "I would like that. Can I help?"

"You want to help cook? Are you sure that's a good idea?"

"Hey, if I'm going to change things about me, I might as well start with cooking, right?"

Evan inhaled sharply, practically hissing. "I don't know. The last time I tried to teach you how to cook, you almost set the counter on fire."

"That's because I didn't know grease is flammable."

"Harvey!"

Harvey cackled and stood up from the couch, wandering lazily toward the tree. He knelt and lifted one of the blue boxes, carrying it back to the couch to Evan.

"Here," he said. "Open your gift before we set the kitchen on fire."

"What's with you and setting things on fire?"

"I just like fire. That's all."

Evan laughed as he unwrapped his gift. His laughter faded as he opened the weathered box and studied the contents.

"Wait, this is..." He shook his head while plucking the floppy disk from the box. "This is ancient. *Indigo Cube?* The last I heard, these things were gone from the internet. How did you find this? It's a rare PC game and—"

"*And* I had it stashed away in my closet for the last Christmas we were together."

"You had this the whole time?"

Harvey blushed as a crooked smirk took his lips. "Well, you served me the divorce papers right around that time. I figured we weren't trading gifts, but I didn't want to get rid of it. I thought...Well, I kind of..."

Evan smiled warmly as he set the gift aside. He cupped Harvey's face, tracing the sleeping bags under Harvey's eyes with his thumbs.

"What did you think?"

Harvey shrugged as his eyes glossed over. "I thought I would save it for a time when we weren't hating each other."

"I can't believe you saved this for me. I've been looking for it for *years*."

"I knew how important it was to you. I mean, I think video games are silly, but I know you treasure them."

Evan sighed shakily, "I love you."

"I love you, too."

"I hate to say it, but I have an overwhelming urge to pop this into my computer upstairs and play it."

Harvey smiled. "Do you want to go do that?"

"No, I want to make you breakfast first."

"Are you sure?"

Evan nodded. "You first. Games later."

"Thank you for doing that."

"I'm going to start cooking. Why don't you grab your gift?"

Harvey shook his head. "I'm supposed to help you cook."

"Go get your gift. I insist."

"All right, fine. But I don't think it'll be better than the gift I got for you."

Evan winked as he stood up from the couch. He walked into the kitchen and started gathering a few pans. After he set them on the stove, he went to the fridge to grab eggs, cream, and bacon. He heated the pans and started adding the ingredients, listening to the sound of wrapping paper being torn.

"This is a small box. Is it a necklace?" Harvey asked.

Evan chuckled. "Open the box, silly."

"I can't imagine what kind of jewelry you would have gotten me. I hardly wear any. I mean..."

As the egg whites turned from clear to white in the pan, Evan cocked his ear in Harvey's direction. The living room was quiet—almost too quiet. He turned curiously to see Harvey standing in front of the island counter with the box held up. Harvey's features were strained to the point that Evan couldn't determine what emotion was trying to surface.

"Harvey? Are you okay?"

Harvey looked at Evan with tears in his eyes. A smile appeared and then turned into a shaky frown. As he attempted to correct his lips, he hiccupped and walked quickly up to Evan's side.

"What's this?"

Evan grinned. "It's your gift."

"But it's a collar and a tag."

"I figured it would be the best compromise for our little problem."

Harvey shook his head. "Evan, are you serious?"

"Yes, I'm more than serious."

"Buster is the worst name for a dog. Did you choose that name?"

Evan laughed. "That was the name on his paperwork. We can always change it if you think of something better."

"I can't believe we're getting a dog."

"I figured it was the best way for me to live out my desire to be a parent and for you to not have to worry so much about raising a tiny human."

Harvey met Evan's gaze tearfully, finally able to fully smile. He shook his head and dove into Evan's chest, burying his face into Evan's sweater. Evan held Harvey for a while until he noticed the eggs needed mixing and the bacon needed turning. He released Harvey to focus on breakfast, nudging Harvey playfully with his shoulder.

"What do you think?"

"I think it's the best gift I've ever gotten."

Evan raised his eyebrows. "And you're okay with it? I know it's abrupt and random, but I thought it could work."

"I think it could work, too."

"What do you say we pick him up after breakfast?"

Harvey nodded excitedly. "That's a great idea."

When Evan finished cooking, he piled two plates full of food. He took them to the coffee table and set the plates next to the cookies, being careful to reposition the glasses of milk as well. Harvey brought a couple of forks to the couch and handed one to Evan.

Evan grinned. "Thanks, baby."

"Merry Christmas, darling."

"Merry Christmas to you."

Harvey laughed. "I can't believe you adopted a *dog*."

"Who says a family has to be humans? We can get a whole bunch of dogs if you want."

"You know you've leveled up as a gay couple when you start adopting pets together."

Evan cackled and shook his head, nearly losing his fork in the process. He lifted his plate and carefully balanced it on his knees.

"I think you're right," he agreed. "I think we also have three years to catch up on."

"I bet we could get it all done by the time I move in."

"I bet so."

Harvey smiled as he turned his attention to his food. He played with his eggs briefly before diving in, humming contentedly with each bite.

"You *have* to tell me how you get the eggs this fluffy," he insisted. "Is it the cream I saw on the counter?"

"Yep, it sure is."

"I have so much to learn."

Evan grinned. "And plenty of time to learn it."

When Evan finished his plate, he sipped his glass of milk. He waited patiently for Harvey to finish and then collected their plates, taking them to the dishwasher. Harvey lingered near the island counter while still clutching the collar in his hand.

"Evan?"

Evan smiled while wiping his hands on a kitchen towel. "Yes, dear?"

"Thank you. For everything."

"No, thank *you*."

Harvey laughed. "What are you thanking me for?"

"For not giving up on a second chance."

"I think we both deserve it."

Evan nodded. "I think so, too. Are you ready to go?"

Harvey glanced down at his plaid pajama pants and his stained t-shirt. He laughed as he shook his head, backing away toward the staircase.

"I'll be right back."

Evan smiled and nodded, walking into the foyer to slip on his boots. He sat on the couch and bent forward to lace his shoes, listening to the sound of the floor creaking above his head. He closed his eyes for a moment and focused on the feeling of warmth around him. The smell of breakfast lingered in the air as well as the sensation that everything had perfectly fallen into place.

"I'm ready."

As Evan opened his eyes, he rose from the couch and strolled toward Harvey, taking Harvey's hand as if they had never spent any time apart. He grabbed his coat, tugged it on, and led Harvey to his car. Once they were safely tucked inside, he drove to the adoption center.

"So, I hear that Buster is a bit of a troublemaker."

"That means we'll get along."

Evan laughed. "Thankfully, Buster doesn't have any thumbs so he can't set anything on fire."

"That's a shame. I could use a crime buddy."

"Am I not your crime buddy?"

Harvey chuckled. "You might qualify."

"And how would I get to qualify more?"

"By sticking around."

Evan turned and winked. "I think I can manage that."

He pulled into the parking lot of the adoption center and parked in the space closest to the door. Harvey bounced from the passenger seat like a puppy, darting toward the door and holding it open for Evan.

Evan shook his head. "You're ridiculous."

"I'm excited. If that's ridiculous, then I'm okay with that."

"I never said it wasn't okay."

Harvey grinned and took Evan's hand as the two of them approached the reception desk.

"Hi, Judy," Evan greeted. "We're here to pick up Buster."

"Hey, Evan! I bet Buster is excited about his new home," she said as she lifted a clipboard. "Why don't you two follow me?"

Harvey squeezed Evan's hand. Evan grinned as they walked down the long hallway toward the back where the kennels were kept. Judy led them to a kennel at the far end that hosted a dark brown German Shephard with tan-brown spots. The dog *yipped* eagerly as Judy unlocked the kennel.

Once the door was open, Buster darted up to Evan and jumped into his arms, causing him to howl with laughter. Harvey tentatively petted Buster's head while Buster continued coating Evan's face with kisses.

Harvey chuckled. "He's got a lot of energy."

"He's two-years-old and he *loves* to play," Judy said. "Do you two have a yard?"

"Oh yes," Evan replied. "Buster is going to love the yard. And we'll take him on hikes, too."

Judy nodded. "He enjoys hiking, too."

"That's excellent," Harvey said. "So, we'll both get some exercise, huh?"

"Do you have his collar?" Evan asked. "I think I have his leash in my pocket."

As Harvey applied Buster's collar, Evan procured the leash from his pocket. He waited until Harvey was done and then attached the leash to Buster's collar, smiling as Buster sat and wagged his tail. The dog didn't seem to want to sit still.

And neither did Evan.

Evan nodded toward the exit. "Are we ready?"

"Definitely," Harvey said with a grin. He turned to Judy and added, "Thank you so much. He's wonderful."

"We're glad to see Buster going to a good family."

"A family," Harvey echoed. "We're a family now, huh?"

"Yes, we are," Evan agreed. "Thanks, Judy. We might be back next year."

Judy laughed. "We look forward to it."

After she led Evan and Harvey back to the front, Evan signed the paperwork releasing Buster and turned to walk Buster and Harvey to the car. Buster hopped into the backseat and Harvey flew in after him, wrapping the dog in a huge hug.

Evan laughed as he shut the door and rounded the car to climb into the driver's seat. He listened to the happy sounds of Harvey cooing in between Buster barking excitedly. When he pulled into the driveway, Harvey led Buster toward the backyard. The two of them disappeared, leaving Evan chuckling on the path leading to the front door.

He wandered inside and set his keys down, leaving his coat on as he walked into the kitchen to locate Buster's toys. He grabbed a rope toy, a squeaky duck, and a tennis ball that he had picked up the day prior in preparation for Buster's arrival. As he waltzed up to the sliding porch door, he watched Harvey jump around the yard with their new dog, smiling warmly as he recognized the happiness radiating from his boyfriend.

This was a good move, he reflected. It works for us both. We don't have to stay apart just because we don't agree. And we don't have to give ourselves up either.

His smile widened as he popped open the door, the squeal of the door on the track alerting Buster. Buster stood at attention with his ears pointed in the air and his fluffy tail stiffened. When he recognized Evan, he barked and sprinted toward Evan, leaping repeatedly to inspect the toys that Evan was carrying.

Evan handed the tennis ball to Harvey. "Give it a go."

"All right, boy. Can you fetch it?"

Harvey tossed the ball across the yard and chuckled as Buster darted after it, chomping down hard on the ball and running back to Harvey to drop it at his feet.

"Wow," he sighed. "I'm impressed!"

Buster barked.

"Do you want to go again?"

Buster whined while focusing on the ball in Harvey's hand. When Harvey tossed it, he chased after it, growling as he shook his head viciously side to side with the ball in his mouth.

"I've got a feeling the furniture will need protecting," Harvey teased. "What do you think, dear?"

"I think you might be right."

"Do you think we'll keep agreeing with each other like this?"

Evan turned to Harvey with a look of mischief, the smile from earlier in the morning still sitting on his lips. It seemed the smile had never left.

"I sure hope not," he replied. "I hope we don't agree on everything because I want us each to have our own opinions. But if we do happen to agree on a lot of things, I'll call that a win."

"You know, despite what our last argument entailed, you have changed in some ways, Evan."

"I can say the same about you."

Harvey wrapped his arms around Evan's shoulders. He kissed Evan softly and sighed as Evan returned the embrace. When he drew back, he peeled his eyes open and smiled warmly, pressing the tip of his nose to Evan's nose.

"I like our family like this," he whispered. "I hope we can keep growing with each other."

"I think we can aim for that."

"So, did I set your heart on fire?"

Evan smirked. "You did so much more than that, Harvey. You lit my whole world on fire."

As Evan leaned into another kiss, his heart exploded with joy. He had retraced the path back to Harvey. He had found a way to reunite that would please them both.

And he intended never to stray again.

www.ingramcontent.com/pod-product-compliance
Lightning Source LLC
Chambersburg PA
CBHW072235150726
48002CB00005B/2096